DISCOVERING RAFE

STRYKER SECURITY FORCE BOOK 5

SARA BLACKARD

ONE

A PING SOUNDED beside Rafe Malone, and he groaned. Not now. Not when victory stood a few clicks away. He jerked his thumb and rapidly pressed the buttons on his controller.

"You're not going to get me today." He flicked his finger as another ping sounded.

He chanced a peek at the flashing icon on one of the computer screens lined on his desk. A smile pushed up his bearded cheeks. Today looked to be a great day.

He turned his focus back to the screen that demanded his priority. His eyes widened as pink flashed on his screen. How the heck did—

"No ..." Rafe frantically pressed buttons, his heart rate increasing. "No, no, no, noooo."

He tossed the controller onto his desk as Princess Peach beat his Mario in the race. He'd been so close, only to lose again.

Story of his life.

"Ha, ha, ha, sucker." The high-pitched voice arrogantly laughed in his earpiece. "Just admit it, old man. You're never gonna beat me, even with this prehistoric game you force me to play."

He leaned close to the video feed on his monitor and gave his sternest look into the camera. "You shouldn't talk to your elders like that."

His niece Sammy tipped back her head and laughed. Her auburn ponytail swayed as the tinkling laughter continued. Rafe leaned back in his office chair and crossed his arms over his chest. His lips twitched to let his smile free as the screen revealed her cheeks pinking with joy.

How could the nine-year-old keep whipping his butt? He'd been playing this stupid game for longer than she'd been alive, yet she beat him every single time. She snorted, sighed, and wiped the tears from beneath her eyes. Rafe found it difficult to keep the straight face.

"Uncle Rafe, you crack me up." Samantha leaned forward so her Pepto-Bismol pink room disappeared from behind her. Her smug expression filled the screen. "What do you think? Best two out of three? Bet I could spank you in those too."

Rafe cocked his eyebrow. "Does your mom know you talk like that?"

"Psh." She leaned back with a smile. "She'd say you deserve it for still playing video games when you're ancient."

"Ancient?" Rafe pointed at her freckled nose. "Ancient? I'll have you know I'm not even thirty yet."

"But you're close." She shrugged and twirled her controller in her hand. "That's ancient. So, what do you say? You game or are you going to tuck your tail and run?"

He let his laugh free and shook his head. "Girl, you are too much. You may have nothing better to do than sit and play games all day, but I have important work that needs to get done."

"Boring." She slumped in her sparkly pink bean bag with a look of utter dejection.

"You better be ready, Sammy." Rafe pointed at her. "I'm going to beat you next time."

"You wish. You always say that, but I only ever see checkered floor in front of me." She sat forward, her face lighting up. "When can we play next?"

"I'll have to text you." The computer pinged again. "Until later, Queen of Mario Kart."

"Farewell, King of Loserville."

"I'm telling." Rafe used his whiny kid voice she always got a kick out of.

Her eyes sparkled as she smiled. "Yeah, right. Then you'd just get a lecture on playing games again."

"You're right." Rafe sighed. His sister could be a real downer sometimes. "Love you, Sam."

"Love you too, Uncle Rafe." She blew him a kiss as he signed off.

Rafe turned to the notification that interrupted his first chance at beating his niece in months. He scowled.

"It's all your fault," he grumbled as he clicked a few icons to pull up the report. A smile spread across his face. "But I guess I'll forgive you."

He'd finally done it. He'd slaved over the last month, working alongside June Rivas, a.k.a. Reagan MacArthur, his friend Sosimo's wife. They'd worked tirelessly trying to figure out how to get her Eyes Beyond tech to work on a larger scale. Her original invention allowed soldiers to have x-ray vision and see beyond the walls and vehicles in front of them. It'd helped them on countless missions and would've saved their friend Ethan Stryker on the mission that changed all their lives if some bureaucrats hadn't screwed them all over.

His hands trembled on the keyboard.

He didn't think about that day.

Ever.

It was the only way he could keep the ghosts away.

He shook his hands out and focused on the data before him. He and June had come up against glitch after glitch as they tried to expand the program. He'd approached her with the idea after a group had strapped a bomb to the underside of the nanny's car. Nothing like some C-4 exploding next to the pond in the backyard to wake one up.

After that little hoopla, he had wanted a way to scan every vehicle, bike, or person who ventured onto their property, and the Eyes Beyond seemed just the ticket. If they could just get it to work, they could minimize the risk to other places besides their own, like The White House, military bases, and embassies. It'd put one more layer of protection between the soldiers and people who guarded those places and the people determined to attack them.

Rafe hooted and lifted his arms up in victory. So what if he couldn't gloat at his niece over a Mario Kart victory? He'd finally figured out what had tripped them up. He grabbed his phone and texted June.

RAFE: I figured it out.

June's reply came quick and to the point.

JUNE: It's working?

He smiled as he typed back.

RAFE: It's running as smooth as a baby's bottom.

Rafe checked his other screens, making sure he had nothing else that needed his attention. The three dots popped up on his phone, indicating June was typing something.

JUNE: You're a stud.

RAFE: I won't tell Sosimo you said that.

An eye-roll emoji appeared, followed by her text.

JUNE: He knows I'm just fluffing your sensitive ego.

RAFE: Woman, there is no fluffing needed here.

JUNE: That's the truth.

Rafe guffawed as he turned in his chair. Sosimo had found an amazing woman when he married June. Sos deserved happiness after everything that had happened. Rafe, on the other hand, didn't deserve to find love. Not after what he'd done. Rafe stood before the memories could crash over him. His phone pinged, and he glanced down.

JUNE: All joking aside, good job, Rafe. I'm so glad we figured out how to make it work. It's going to help so much.

Rafe moved his fingers to type back when his phone rang. His forehead furrowed. Restricted number?

"Hello? Rafe here."

"Rafe? It's Davis." His best friend's voice sounded strained.

"Davis, you on leave, or what?" Rafe couldn't believe it'd been so long since he'd talked to his childhood friend. Since he'd left the Army, he and Davis didn't have the chance to cross paths like they used to.

Rafe logged out of his personal computer and left to go to the kitchen and grab a snack.

"No, getting ready to leave on an extended mission. Listen, I need your help. Chloe and Piper are in some kind of trouble." Davis's agitation grew.

"What do you mean?"

"Some dude has been leaving strange messages for Chloe down in Texas." He huffed. "They're up in Steamboat Springs for a concert and just found a note taped to their door." He growled. "Rafe, you should've heard how scared they sounded."

"Dude, I'll leave right now. I'll be there in less than an hour." Rafe rushed out of the room.

"Man, thank you. I'm glad you're there." Davis's sigh sounded as if it came all the way from his toes. "I'm tired of being so far away, Rafe. Think I might be ready to follow you out and be done with the military."

"We could always use another hand here." Rafe took the stairs two at a time. He'd do anything for the Fields family. He'd spent as much time or more at Davis's aunt and uncle's house, where Davis and Piper lived after their parents died. They were like family. "Don't worry, Davis. I won't let anything happen to the girls."

"Thanks, man. I'll call when I can."

"Keep your head down." Rafe shoved his phone in his pocket after Davis agreed and hung up.

Rafe strode into the office, interrupting Zeke Greene and his wife Samantha from kissing. Rafe would've cracked a joke about interoffice relationships, but he didn't have time to screw around. Samantha jumped away from Zeke and placed her fingers over her cheeks before straightening her hair.

Rafe couldn't help himself. "Stop making out. We've got some serious business here."

"Knock much?" Zeke scowled as he flexed his fingers.

"Hey. If you want privacy, close the door." Rafe pointed his thumb behind him at the open doorway. "Listen, I need to go to Steamboat, and I need to take your plane."

"Okay." Zeke crossed his arms. "What's going on?"

"Just got a call from Davis. His cousin and sister have a stalker issue. His cousin is performing in Steamboat this weekend." Rafe ran a hand over his beard and tugged. "The dude followed them up there from Texas. Left a note on their door."

"Take Jake. He's a better pilot."

Rafe nodded and headed for the door. Zeke was right. Jake could fly a plane through the eye of a needle if it fit.

"I'll send you the girls' info so you can call them," Rafe called over his shoulder. "Tell them to hang tight until we get there."

Rafe didn't wait for a response. Zeke knew what to do. Rafe pictured Piper and Chloe the last time he'd seen them. Five or six years had to have passed since he had gone back with Davis for the girls' high school graduation.

Back then Chloe had just gotten out of the hospital and still had the dark shadows on her face of someone who'd gone to hell and back. Piper had smiled from ear to ear, still swimming in the oversized shirts she always wore. She had changed little since they'd first moved into the neighborhood when she was twelve. He remembered laughing at how she'd looked back and forth between him, Davis, and Chloe, like at any moment one of them might disappear.

Piper had always been a worrier. Rafe couldn't imagine how crazed she must be with all of this. He'd not only keep the girls safe, but he'd also find out who this creep was. Piper didn't need any more worry piled on her shoulders. Rafe picked up his pace. He couldn't get to Steamboat fast enough.

Piper Fields stared at the full-length mirror in the bath-room of the house they'd rented. The garnet sweater didn't hug her tight and expose her fluff, but also didn't fit her like a circus tent. It somehow accentuated her body in ways she never thought possible. She should go back and buy every sweater they had in her size.

She still couldn't believe she'd allowed Chloe, her cousin and America's next country music darling, to talk her into a shopping spree. She had to admit, though, that the new clothes gave her a boost in confidence. Maybe she could even consider accepting Chloe's newest guitarist's, Chet Stevens, invitations to dinner. Piper's hands slicked with sweat and her mouth went dry. Then again, maybe she wasn't ready for that yet.

Her old clothing had become a security blanket. The habit had sprouted from her grief when her parents had died in a car accident. It had buried thick, deep roots when her aunt and uncle enrolled her into private school with Chloe. Her looming height and fleshy frame hadn't exactly fit in with the petite, anorexic image toted by the popular crowd.

She still could hear the teasing barbs the girls would throw about how school uniforms didn't work on Wookiees, like Piper had any say in how tall she grew. Or that she hadn't learned to tame her hair that wasn't curly, but also wasn't straight until well into her sophomore year. By then the damage had been done and the jock guys would make Wookiee calls when she passed in the hall. Her relief at missing most of their senior year because she refused to leave Chloe at the hospital by herself had been so selfish. She still felt guilty of being glad to have an excuse to not go to school.

Her mother had always claimed Piper would be a great warrior princess, like all her Viking ancestors from the stories her mother had told. Piper had dreamed of Nordic fairytales growing up. Of being tall and beautiful, just like her mother. Instead, she'd ended up more a frumpy giant than the gorgeous goddess her mom had been.

Piper adjusted the tunic sweater and yanked the hem a little more over the leggings, smoothing down the soft fabric. The deep red of the knit brought out the pink in her cheeks and made her green eyes pop. *Huh.* She cocked her head to the side. She never thought about how the dreary clothes she wore could make her look tired.

Turning one more time in front of the mirror, she smiled. Maybe there was a bit of her mother in her after all. She rolled her eyes, headed back to the living room, and slumped on to the couch, glancing at her watch. The security team Davis had suggested should be there soon. According to Zeke Greene, Davis's friend and owner of the firm, it would take a little over an hour for his men, Jake and Rafe, to get there. Only fifteen minutes had passed since they'd gotten off the phone, but Piper swore more like forty had.

Her stomach had twisted when Zeke had said the name Rafe. It pretzeled thinking about it again. Rolling her neck, she reached up and rubbed the knot between her shoulders. Zeke couldn't be talking about Rafe Malone, Davis's best friend from high school. Surely Davis would've told her if Rafe had gotten out of the Army.

That she still crushed on her brother's best friend after not seeing him for six years and nine months merely proved that she lived a pathetic life. What kind of person kept a secret flame going for that long? Chloe was the only one who knew Piper had pined for the unattainable back in high school.

She hoped she hadn't been obvious in her insistence of keeping that crush alive after so many years. None of her handful of dates since getting out of high school had come remotely close to measuring up to Rafe. She hoped that fact didn't prove she was destined to be alone for life.

She shook her head and snatched a tourist magazine from the coffee table, mad at herself for letting her mind travel down the road to Rafeville yet again.

Muffled muttering and a crash sounded from upstairs. Had Chloe lost something again? The note taped to the front door came to mind, picking up her heart rate. Piper lowered the magazine as she peered up the stairs.

"Chloe, you okay?" Piper hollered.

"I'm good." Chloe sounded out of breath. "Just doing some wardrobe adjustments. I'll be right down."

Piper snorted as she flipped a page she hadn't looked at. Chloe was always adjusting her concert sets, whether it was her wardrobe, her dancing, or something else Piper didn't realize needed adjusting. Chloe would freak if she knew that Piper still harbored her childhood dream of becoming a stay-at-home mom like her mother had been. Chloe had nearly gone into seizures when they'd talked about their dreams of the future one night under the covers.

Even at fourteen, Chloe had wanted to be a country music star. When Piper had said she just wanted to be a wife and mom and homeschool her kids, Chloe had spazzed out about women being liberated from such nonsense until she'd collapsed into an exhausted heap. Piper hadn't ever said anything about it again, but in her heart, that dream still held tight. Not that it looked to come true anytime soon, if ever.

Her mom had been the most amazing woman she had ever known, not only strong but so happy it beamed from her. Why couldn't Piper dream of a happiness like her mother's? Of course, if she never dated, then she'd never find a husband to build a happy home with.

Chloe tripped down the stairs with an armful of Piper's old clothes. Piper's stomach twisted. What was her cousin up to now? Their security guards would be there in—Piper glanced at her watch—about thirty-five minutes. She'd just finished straightening the place.

"What are you doing?" Piper tried not to act perturbed as she flipped a page in the magazine.

"Bonfire. Remember?" Chloe's bright smile slid ice down Piper's back.

"Now?" Piper stood, her voice coming out like a squeak. She figured with the whole stalker issue that Chloe would forget all about their agreement to burn Piper's old clothes.

"Yep."

Piper should've known that Chloe wouldn't let it go. She probably worried that Piper would fall back into the habit of wearing the old sacks of monotone dreary. But still, the bodyguards could be there any minute.

"But what about the note? Shouldn't we stay inside and wait for Zeke's guys?" She stood and prepared to take her clothes back upstairs.

Chloe tossed the clothes on the entry floor and rushed back upstairs. Obviously, the men showing up didn't worry her cousin. Piper placed her hands on her hips and stared at the one tone pile of ugly. Why had she wrapped herself in that for so long?

Probably the same reason she'd held onto her crush on Rafe Malone for years. Maybe it was time to light the whole mess on fire, toss her silly infatuation in the flames as well. She needed to let that go, burn it on the pyre of childish dreams and insecurities. She'd never find the happy life her mom had loved so much if she didn't at least try, and a hot guitarist might prove the perfect first step into embracing that legacy her mother claimed Piper came from. She scooped up the clothes and stomped with purpose to the fire pit.

TWO

RAFE TAPPED his fingers on the console of the rental SUV as Jake drove them to the house. Maybe he should've insisted on driving so he could think about something other than getting to the girls to keep them safe. He was most likely overreacting, but it was like his own sisters were in trouble.

Both of his siblings had been older, and his brother, being the oldest, had been ten-years-old when Rafe was born. Growing up, he had learned not to count on his siblings for playmates. But having Davis's baby sister and cousin always hanging around had given Rafe that sense of siblings that were close. At first, it had weirded Rafe out that Davis didn't care that his sister tagged along, but then it added to the fun, two more playmates that liked to laugh at his jokes and squeal when he chased them. Maybe losing their parents had made Davis and Piper so close, but Rafe had envied their relationship.

Now the thought of Chloe being in trouble, and knowing Piper stuck to her cousin like glue, had all his protective genes firing. He couldn't imagine what Davis was thinking right now, being stuck on assignment and not able to come help Piper. Hopefully Davis's mission was a more exciting one rather than those missions that had hours and days that stretched into boring sameness, giving a soldier lots of time to gnaw on worries.

"Man, would you stop fidgeting?" Jake looked at Rafe like he'd grown two heads. "You're driving me nuts."

"Sorry." Rafe balled his fingers into his palm and concentrated on keeping his edgy nerves from bouncing his leg.

"What's with you? You're acting weird ... well, weirder." Jake scowled at the road before him.

"I don't know, man." Rafe speared his hand through his hair, then quickly fixed it. "Davis's sister and cousin are like my little sisters. I guess I haven't been able to relax since Davis called all panicky."

"Well, knock it off." Jake gripped the steering wheel.

Rafe breathed deep and scanned the upscale neighborhood that edged the ski slope. The houses, while beautiful, were built so close together it left little privacy. It also provided a stalker with the ability to get close with little effort at all.

"This neighborhood is a security nightmare." Rafe huffed and pounded his hand on the door.

Jake grunted his agreement.

"We need to find another place to stay, one we can have more control over." Rafe scanned the townhouses and mini-mansions for a sleaze ball hiding out in the shrubs.

"Call Zeke. Get him on it."

Rafe jumped at the task but wished Jake would put a little more pressure on the gas pedal. When the call connected, he relayed the information to Zeke and hung up. Within the next few hours, they should have a place they could keep the girls nice and protected in.

Jake pulled into the driveway behind a little sports car that screamed Chloe. Rafe opened the door before the vehicle stopped and scanned the area. The other houses had security cameras, so hopefully one of them caught something they could use.

He pointed to the closest house. "We'll have to see about getting access to those security feeds."

"Since all these rentals are run by one housing company, maybe the feeds will be connected on one system."

"Maybe." Rafe let Jake take the lead up the stairs while he kept his eyes peeled for someone or something out of place.

Jake knocked on the door, and, after what seemed like an eternity, footsteps approached the door. Rafe's shoulders relaxed. They'd get in, secure the girls, then get them to a better location. Once there, he could work his magic on the computer and track this guy down.

"What's the password?" Chloe's voice through the door caused Rafe to smile, reminding him of all the times they'd gone to their fort in the woods behind the Fields's house. Even when they'd been in high school, the four of them would still hang out in that rickety fort overlooking the pond.

Jake cleared his throat. "Butterfingers and potbelly pigs."

Rafe snorted. Their old password sounded ridiculous coming from Jake's lips. That was so worth making him take the lead. If Rafe had been thinking, he would've videoed it. Then he could add it to the gag reels he pulled out when he wanted to make the guys suffer. He'd collected some good ones over the years.

Jake speared him with a glare before turning forward as the door swung open. Jake tensed beside him. Chloe stood there gaping at Jake like she had that one time the high school star quarterback came home with Rafe and Davis to hang out. She'd had the biggest crush on him, and Davis and Rafe had teased her for days after. Rafe smirked. Looked like things hadn't changed that much. She still gawked at guys.

Rafe needed to get this starefest over with. "Chloe?"

"Rafe?" Her surprised voice eased into his cracks, bringing back all those childhood memories.

He swooped her into a hug, careful not to squeeze too hard. She hadn't changed a bit. She still had her hair cut short like Tinkerbell and was way too skinny. She couldn't help it, but it still made him want to handle her like a china doll. If she knew that, she'd throw a left hook at his face.

"Think we can move this reunion inside?" Jake's extra gruff voice sounded annoyed.

He'd have to get over it. This was family. No straight-laced security job this time. He adjusted his hug and picked Chloe off her feet with a growl and stepped inside the house.

Movement drew his eyes to the living room where a woman leaned against the couch. Her red sweater melted onto her tall frame and caused his chest to pound like one of those cartoon characters with their hearts pumping out of their bodies. His eyes widened as he realized this was no stranger, but Piper Fields. He swallowed. When'd she grown up?

"Pipster?" Was that his voice?

"Hey, Rafe. Long time, no see." Piper's soft words slid across his nerves and made him shiver.

Get with it, man. This was Davis's kid sister.

"Too long, it seems." Rafe forced his feet to unfreeze and crossed the room.

He pulled her into a hug, but couldn't seem to think clearly. Florals, citrus, and something he'd never smelled before picked up his heart rate and made him want to bury his nose deep into her hair. Her tall frame fit perfect in his arms. What in the world? His brotherly feelings flew right out the window. *Davis's sister, Malone. Completely off limits.*

He pulled back and tried for a teasing smile. "You look amazing. Davis would flip a brick if he saw you now."

Her big brown eyes widened, and a blush crept into her cheeks. Wow. Davis's sister. Right. Rafe took a step back.

"Do I smell smoke?" Jake's question brought Rafe to alert.

The tinge of smoke overlaid Piper's intoxicating scent. He gently squeezed her arm then stepped around her, heading straight to the porch door. Flames licked the pergola and engulfed a pile of clothes. Rapid footsteps and hushed whispers preceded the cousins as Chloe half-rushed, half-sauntered out like she always had when she was hiding something.

"Are those underwear?" Jake tipped his head to the side.

Rafe leaned forward to get a better view of the clothes piled in the fire pit. Sure enough, underwear topped the pile. Out of his peripheral, Piper's shoulders slumped. So this was her little bonfire. Interesting. Chloe plopped more clothes on top of the pile, smothering the fire from flames to smoke.

"Why are you two burning clothes? Some sort of demonstration or something?" Rafe coughed and waved the smoke from his face.

One thing hadn't changed. These two were still trouble. He moved closer to Piper to get out of the fumes.

"It's a ceremonial pyre celebrating change." Chloe grinned impishly at him.

"What change?" The question broke loose something primal in him.

He turned to Piper and scanned her up and down. Why did she want to change? She stared into the fire, her arms crossed over her chest.

"Well ..." Chloe sure was the same as always. Her face still had that look that she was coming up with a story. "We didn't bring the right type of clothes for the Colorado cold, so we got new ones."

"You got new underwear for the Colorado cold?" Rafe snorted. What a ridiculous thought.

She crossed her arms and cocked her eyebrow. "No, we found this store with some sexy bits of lace we couldn't pass up. No use keeping the cotton ones when you've got pretties to wrap yourself in. Though, I guess it's not really wrapping since there's not much fabric there to begin with."

She cocked her head to the side and gave him a demure smile. His brain froze and his body heated. He pulled at his coat, the material suddenly toasty.

That meant ... he peeked over at Piper. She stared into the fire, her fingers rubbing the neckline of her sweater. He couldn't stop staring as he thought of the way she smelled. Jake rumbled something, and Rafe shook his head to clear his hearing.

Chloe threw her arms wide and, in typical Chloe-style, took center stage. "Sacrifices to the Goddess of Fashion, petitioning her for marvelous fits that drive men—"

The flames flashed with a loud whoosh. Rafe pushed Piper behind him. Her hands flattened on his back, and warmth spread through his shoulders. She blew out a breath that skittered along the back of his neck, raising all of his hair. *What the heck?* Her closeness had his body overheating and his mind spinning.

"I think she heard you, Chloe." Piper laughed and stepped back next to him, her hand trailing across his shoulder.

Drive men wild. That's what Chloe was about to say. Rafe peeked at Piper as she wiped tears of laughter from her eyes. The goddess had not only heard, but answered. He inwardly groaned and turned back to the fire. *Davis's sister. Davis's sister.* He'd just have to remember to keep up his chant, otherwise the Bro Code might get chucked into the snowbank.

Piper excused herself from the bonfire of embarrassment and misery to get some distance from Rafe. *Lord, why?* She pleaded in her head. How could Rafe have gotten even more good-looking since the last time she'd seen him?

She liked that he'd grown his hair out and slicked it back. His well-groomed beard had surprised her. He'd always been meticulous about his appearance, which just added to that magnetic manliness that drew her. She wondered if the beard would tickle if she kissed him.

She huffed in disgust at herself and stomped into the kitchen. She would not let herself spiral into this obsession again. She had declared herself done with this nonsense not fifteen minutes ago. Of course, her resolve just had to be tested with his larger-than-life arrival.

Piper took the lid off the stew and stirred with vigor. Why did he have to show up while the bonfire still blared? She tilted her head back and groaned. What had possessed her to toss her granny panties right on top? Then for Chloe to make that comment. She shook her head, remembering how Rafe had scrutinized her like she was a bug under a magnifying glass. Oh, how she'd tried not to fidget under his scrutiny.

Piper slammed the spoon on to the holder and turned toward the fridge. Maybe if she hid herself in here, she could just avoid contact with Rafe. She pulled out the makings for a salad and grabbed some mushrooms she could stuff for appetizers. She knew the hideout wouldn't last forever, but maybe it would give her enough time to build that resolve back up.

She grabbed the knife and cutting board and chopped the lettuce. She just needed to remember why it would never work between her and Rafe. Maybe then her heart wouldn't betray her and speed her down that road she no longer wanted to drive on.

Okay, what were the reasons a relationship would never happen with Rafe Malone?

Reason number one: He was Davis's best friend. Wasn't there some kind of stupid code guys had about dating their friends' sisters?

Reason number two: He just saw her as a little sister. She rolled her eyes at all the times she'd prayed that he would notice her, only to have him rub his knuckles on her head.

Reason number three: She was a grown woman, not a silly teenage girl. She didn't have to hold on to pubescent crushes anymore.

Reason number four: They had totally different lives now. It'd be smarter for her to throw her attention on someone like Chet. At least then she'd be able to spend time with him during their busy schedule.

She closed her eyes and tried to bring up a picture of Chet, but all she got was Rafe as he smiled down at her and the strength in his arm as he'd pulled her behind him.

Reason number ... what number was she on? Ugh, it didn't matter. There was no way Rafe would ever find her attractive. Men like him didn't go for Wookiees. Her chopping slowed as Chet's repeated invitations out came to mind.

Men like Chet didn't usually go for her either. Her hands shook, so she set the knife down and pushed her hands through her hair. She glanced down at her outfit, then toward the living room. Rafe had seemed shocked when he saw her, his expression going from a look she'd seen men give Chloe all the time to disbelief.

Had she changed that much since high school? She shook her head. She didn't think so. She was still the same old Piper, more comfortable making things happen behind the scenes than being the one in the spotlight.

She kept makeup simple and her hair long and boring. She supposed the only thing that had really changed was her outfits and that was a recent development. Which meant Rafe's attention wouldn't change either. She looked down at her heart and poked it.

"Don't be stupid. You hear me?" Please let her heart listen.

Rafe's partner walked through the living room and out the front door. Piper jerked back to work. If she could play it cool, she could get through the next few days without any more embarrassment. Rafe and Chloe's laughter filtered into the kitchen from the porch. His still held the joy that always made her heart expand in her chest every time she heard it. Too bad for her he liked to laugh.

"You're not a teenage girl, but a woman," she muttered to herself as she tossed onions into a saute pan to brown. "Rafe is first and foremost a friend. Don't screw that up and make things awkward by being a ninny."

She added sausage to the onions. As that cooked, she cleaned the mushrooms. She would do this and prove to herself once and for all that she could behave like the woman she had become, the woman who worked tirelessly to push her cousin's career into stardom.

It's what she and Chloe had talked about for hours in the hospital their senior year. It's what Piper had spent the last six years researching, studying, and transforming herself into a promoting machine to men and women that could give them their next big break or slam the door tightly shut in their faces. Managing Chloe was demanding and fulfilling, and Piper did a great job at it. She just needed to translate the confidence she had in her job to her ability to manage her attraction.

She squared her shoulders. She could do this. She'd just slide those emotions she'd tied to Rafe into the back of her mind, just like she slid her jumble of nerves when she was contacting recording studios. If it worked then, it would work now.

His laugh sounded again from outside, and her heart jumped. Maybe. Hopefully. Her twisted stomach didn't agree with her head.

THREE

"CHLOE, I can't believe we let you talk us into this."
Rafe laughed as he shook his head and stared out the front window of the vehicle at hot air balloons being set up.

He didn't know when she'd scheduled the balloon rides. She'd been busy with threatening notes, panty bonfires, and packing her hundred pounds of clothes for the move. Somewhere in all of that, she had called and set up an early morning balloon ride.

"It's going to be amazing. Just you wait." Chloe opened her door and got out.

Jake followed, but Piper didn't. Rafe had been hyper-aware of everything that Piper had been doing since he got here the day before. Little things like the way she had chopped vegetables deftly with her long, slender fingers, her throaty laugh that had never spiraled in his belly before, or how her eyes twinkled when Chloe told stories of what they'd been up to the last six years.

She'd walk past, and whatever perfume she wore

would tease up his nostrils and zap his brain cells. It was like the stuff was made to lure him in, then hook him in the mouth. Except he, being the idiot he was, swallowed the entire stinking hook.

Davis's sister. Davis's sister.

The chant didn't work well.

When she'd come down for a glass of water in her PJ pants and t-shirt the night before, he'd about said some stupid joke. Yet, when he'd looked up from the computer screen in his search for the stalker, her make-up free face and hair knotted in a messy bun had dried all joking up in his throat. Brain cells evaporated and leaked out his ear.

She was gorgeous—a goddess. He would've bowed at her feet and kissed her teal painted toenails if his brain hadn't shut down in a full system failure. Which saved him from doing something stupid like slipping her hair from the knot to see if it would slide through his fingers like water.

He shook his head. *Davis's sister. Act normal.*

"Pipster, everything okay?" He turned in the seat to look at her.

Her hair flowed down her back from under her stocking hat, the deep brown contrasting with the light blue of her winter coat. She'd put some make-up on, not much, but just enough to draw attention to her dark brown eyes that had flecks of gold in the center. How had he never noticed how beautiful she was? Because he shouldn't be noticing that kind of stuff.

"Great. Just staying warm a few seconds more." She

smiled, though it looked forced, and pushed the door open.

Rafe stepped out and rounded the vehicle. The crisp, cool air cleared his head. He scanned the bushes and open field, but came up empty. This actually might be one of Chloe's better plans. They'd spend an hour or so up in the air, far from any danger, then head back to the house for the rest of the day. Let Chloe feel like she wasn't trapped while experiencing the killer Steamboat views.

Piper pointed with her coffee cup between the two balloons. "Looks like someone else is going up too."

Rafe looked down the road to see if anyone was driving up.

"Actually, I booked both of them." Chloe cringed and pointed her chin at the balloon closest to them "I didn't realize the baskets were that big."

Piper's head whipped back to the balloons, glancing between the two of them. Rafe smirked and shook his head. Typical Chloe, never thinking things through all the way.

"We'll cancel one of them." Jake's words echoed Rafe's thoughts.

Chloe rolled her eyes. "That would be silly. They're already paid for. Besides, it would be rude to cancel now after they've already set up."

Rafe stepped to the door and double-checked his pack. Chloe would wheedle Jake into agreeing. She'd always been able to talk her way into things. Not in the spoiled brat kind of way, but more like she was just so sweet people ended up wanting to agree with her.

He glanced over and barely stifled his snort. She had leaned up against Jake, her eyes batting like a tornado whipped them. Jake just stared down at her, his Adam's apple bobbing. Huh. Maybe the little firecracker had lit old Grumpy Butt's fuse. His friend needed that, needed to realize that his injuries didn't have to be the end of his dreams.

Rafe smiled as he slung on his backpack. He'd go along with Chloe's ridiculous idea. A little balloon ride might be just what the doctor ordered for Jake.

The women walked toward the balloons, so Rafe stepped up next to Jake. "That Chloe, she's sure got spunk. Always has."

Jake grunted. "Wish she would've talked to us before planning this."

"Come on, man. This will get those trapped jitters out, then we'll be back to the house before most of the morning is gone."

Rafe glanced at Piper and Chloe. They turned and looked at him. He smiled and nodded, then shook his head when they snapped their heads back around. Those two were up to something. He could tell.

One of the workers approached the women. A smile grew on the dude's face as Piper talked animatedly with her hands. He was the epitome of cool with his hair curling around the bottom of his knit cap and his relaxed stature screaming Colorado outdoor fun. The man reached out his hand, and Piper took it. What in the world? Rafe's muscles tightened and legs stomped toward her before he realized he moved.

"What's he doing?" Rafe practically barked the question at Chloe.

Get a hold of yourself, man. He crossed his arms over his chest, but couldn't control the scowl pushing his eyebrows together. Piper laughed about something the guy said, and Rafe wanted to growl, maybe rip the guy's arms from his limbs.

"Piper's a little nervous about going up, so that nice-looking guy is showing her about the balloon to ease her mind." Chloe interrupted his thoughts of dismemberment.

"He's not so nice looking." Rafe smoothed his hand over his hair. Why had he just said that?

"Listen, Rafe, Piper's pretty scared about this." Chloe's voice filled with concern.

"Pipster? She loves rides." She'd always begged to go to the carnival every time it came to town to enjoy the rides, even the ones that had him clenching his butt cheeks.

"Yeah, I know. Surprised me, too. Do you think you can keep an eye on her while you're up there? I don't want her to pass out or anything."

He nodded and rubbed his hands together. He'd make sure she had a great ride. "Yeah, I'll keep a real close eye on her."

Chloe smiled big, like he was a hero or something. Not likely.

"Thanks, Rafe." Chloe's mood turned serious. "I'm glad you're here. Piper takes on so much. It'll be good for her to have a little Rafe magic around."

Rafe rubbed the ache in his chest and nodded. Rafe magic? He didn't think it still existed. Maybe a mirage of who he'd been waved and tricked others into believing it was there. But where before being the jokester had been embedded in his skin, now he joked to keep people from realizing that his last mission had tainted him to his very soul.

Rafe shook off the thought and focused on Piper. The man stared at her like she was a box of filled donuts he hadn't expected he'd get. Rafe got that. Piper had grown into an amazing woman. Why hadn't anyone snatched her up yet? The thought of her married twisted his gut.

When Piper stepped up next to them, Rafe put his arm over her shoulder and looked down at her. He meant it in a brotherly action to comfort her, but couldn't trick his mind off the chest-thumping action that it was. The rise of the balloon worker's eyebrows showed he understood the action.

"You okay?" Rafe breathed in her scent.

Piper ducked her head and shrugged. "I am now."

What did that mean?

"All right, I think we are ready to go. You two will be in the far balloon." Balloon guy pointed to Piper and Rafe. "I'll be your pilot."

"Great," Rafe muttered as Piper smiled.

He didn't move his arm until she stepped toward the balloon. She fit next to him perfectly with her tall height. No slumping required to hold her close. He shouldn't even contemplate things like that. Nothing could ever come of an attraction to her. Davis would kill him, but, more importantly, he didn't deserve someone after what he'd had to do, especially someone as pure and giving as Piper.

They climbed into the basket and lifted off. He kept his mind focused and trained on the snowy ground below where an attack would come if it did. He just had to remember that she was his friend, practically family, and that his mind needed to keep that fact firmly set.

"Rafe?" Her trembling voice drew his attention from the shadows of the brush below.

Piper's hands clenched the side of the basket so hard her entire fingers turned white. She had her eyes squeezed closed and her breath came in quick bursts. Chloe wasn't joking about catching Piper if she fainted.

"Hey, Pip, it's fine." He placed his hand over hers.

"No." She was going to hyperventilate.

"Piper, look at me."

She shook her head.

Rafe wrapped his arm around her and pulled her close. He touched his hand to her chin and tipped her head up. Dear Lord, she took his breath away.

"Piper, please look at me."

She blinked, her pained eyes filled with unshed tears. "I'm sorry. I'm being stupid."

"Shh, you're fine." Better than fine. He swallowed. "Did Davis ever tell you about the time in basic when he somehow unbuckled his belt, and his pants dropped to his ankles in front of the entire squadron?"

She gasped, her eyes going wide with amusement. "He didn't." She placed her hand over Rafe's heart.

Warmth filled his chest and flooded his core. He should have let her go as he told story after story during the ride to distract her. He really should have. Yet her laughter filled his chest so he could finally breathe. For the first time in two years, he felt like himself. So, he kept his arms around her and told himself he'd remember all the reasons he couldn't be with her when they landed.

FOUR

THE NEXT DAY Piper sat beside Rafe at Ellie Smithton's house. Chloe's fan had gushed on and on about how amazing Chloe was. Piper had stood off to the side, cherishing this moment for her cousin. Now, several hours later, she and Rafe leaned their backs against the kitchen island as they waited for the meeting to finish.

He shifted, and his arm brushed against hers. She told her heart to knock it off as it tripped and stuttered into top gear. It'd been doing that since Rafe had held her in his arms and distracted her with stories during the disastrous balloon ride. She always knew she hated tight spaces, but never realized enormous balloons too. Yep, utter disaster.

Disastrous because she not only made a fool of herself, but now had her mind thinking all kinds of daydreams that rivaled any she'd ever been able to conjure before. The dam she'd built against her pitiful crush had broken wide open. It was like being held in his wonderful arms with his citrus and leather scent filling her senses and weakening her knees had knocked all her defenses loose.

Then she had to go and slip on ice outside the Smithton's house. Rafe had caught her, just slipped his arms around her back and kept her from crashing to the cement like she didn't weigh a ton. Okay, a ton was dramatic, but still. She wasn't one of those willowy, tall girls, and he'd caught her like she was. His forehead had gotten that adorable crease it got when he worried, which wasn't often.

She remembered it clearly from the time he'd found her hiding in the high school library. It was the only year they shared in high school. She had been beyond embarrassed to think he might have known the teasing had been particularly cruel that day. He'd probably already known everyone called her a Wookiee, but she didn't want to come right out and say it if by some miracle he hadn't.

So she had lied, told him she'd failed a test in geometry. For once her misery hadn't been a complete waste, since he told her he'd tutor her. Though she hadn't needed the tutoring with her ninety-eight percent in the class and had felt slightly guilty about taking an hour of his time three days a week, she'd kept up tutoring the entire year.

Piper shifted, letting her arm press against his. His look of concern as he'd caught her on the driveway had brought even more memories and emotions to the surface. Too bad she couldn't get him to tutor her on walking.

Piper peeked at his profile and whipped her gaze away, wiping her sweaty palms on her jeans. She tried to play it cool. Oh, how she tried. With the way her mind and heart raced since he showed up, she worried at any moment she'd slip up and confess her undying love to him.

She didn't need this, not with all Chloe had going on. Piper's focus should be on making sure everything went smoothly and that Chloe stayed safe. It definitely shouldn't be on the heat that radiated off of Rafe's arm or the desire to lean her head on his shoulder.

Maintaining the illusion of childhood friends just about zapped her already flagging energy. She'd need a nap when they got back to the rental. Maybe a nice cold shower to shock her sensibilities back to normal.

"Ellie, it was so nice to meet you." Chloe pulled Ellie in for a hug.

Piper stood faster than necessary, needing action, needing to get her brain thinking about all Chloe had to do this week instead of zeroing in on everything Rafe. Her head spun with the rush of blood, and she swayed.

"Whoa, Turbo, where's the fire?" Rafe wrapped his hand gently around her arm, then pulled it away like she'd shocked him.

"Sorry." She averted her gaze and followed Chloe to the door.

For Pete's sake, she was pathetic. No wonder she hadn't had a date in years. *You'd have plenty of dates if they didn't have to measure up to Rambo Rafe.* One guy in particular who was not only kind and smart but good looking. That was it. She was taking Chet up on his invitation to dinner after they got back to Texas.

"Here, let me help you across the ice." Rafe slid his arm around her waist.

She inwardly groaned with the unfairness of it all. Why couldn't Davis have called a different friend? Rafe tightened his grip on her waist, and she both loved and loathed the feeling.

"Rafe," Jake's voice snapped in front of them.

The next thing she knew, Rafe smashed her into the corner of the house and garage with a shaken Chloe huddled next to her. Piper couldn't see a thing except Rafe's back.

"What is it?" Her question squeaked out.

"A note on the windshield." Chloe's voice trembled.

The pressure of being pushed against the house and the trembling of Chloe next to Piper had her skin crawling and her throat closing in on her. Trapped. She felt trapped and wanted out.

"Rafe." She pushed on his shoulder.

"Hold." Rafe leaned back further.

Could one suffocate while in open air? The confining space tried its best to do it. *Oh God, please don't let me pass out.*

"Rafe, I need out. I need out." She pushed harder on him, her breath coming quick and short and not helping her at all.

He shifted forward and wrapped his arm back around her. "Shh, Pip. I know. I'll let you out as soon as it's safe."

She laid her forehead on his back, trying desperately to slow her breathing. Of course he knew. He'd been the one to find her when they were playing ultimate hide and seek. The old, hollowed-out log she'd chosen for a hiding spot had collapsed on her, pinning her in the dark confines for what had seemed a lifetime. He'd had to hold her for a good five minutes before she had calmed down enough to go to the house. Ever since then, the thought of being trapped freaked her out.

She drew in a deep breath, his leather scent soothing her unraveling nerves. If she leaned on him, maybe her fear wouldn't wrap its sticky tentacle around her heart and pull her to the miry pit of anxiety that would drown her. She laid her cheek between his shoulders and pressed her body against his back. She filled her lungs with his scent, opening her mouth so she not only smelled but tasted it.

The next breath came with less effort. She opened her eyes and found Chloe frozen, staring at the vehicle. Her cousin's fear slithered into her own, and Piper slammed her eyes back closed. *Selfish.* How could she be so selfish?

She swallowed and forced her fear down. Peeling her eyelids open, she reached out and grabbed Chloe's hand. Her cousin squeezed Piper's palm like her life depended on it. This creep had pushed too far.

"We're good," Jake said as he reached past Rafe and grabbed Chloe.

Rafe adjusted his grip on Piper and pulled her next to him. They rushed to the vehicle door, Rafe half-carrying her the entire way. She couldn't help but stare at the paper flapping under the wiper like it was taunting them. Rafe lifted her into the back seat and ran his hand down her cheek.

"You okay?" His voice came out tight and gruff.

Lying, she nodded and swiveled her legs into the car.

She wasn't cut out for this. This situation had her throat closing tight, and the guy wasn't even her stalker. She shook her head and pushed her hair away from her face. Maybe getting serious about dating and finding someone to share a life with wasn't such a bad idea. Her dream of a June Cleaver life with her mother's charismatic twist looked better each second terror gripped her heart and squeezed.

Could she leave Chloe to her music career alone? Piper peeked at Chloe's trembling hands and knew she couldn't. Her worry for Chloe would probably keep her close to her side, which meant June Cleaver would have to stay locked away with the rest of her daydreams.

"What does it say?" Chloe's voice trembled, completely unlike her strong cousin.

Rafe scanned the note. His cheek clenched like when he would keep something from her and Chloe growing up. He glanced over at Jake, just like he used to glance at Davis. Piper wouldn't let him go all secretive with them now.

"Rafe?" Piper surprised herself with her firm tone.

Rafe cleared his throat and read. "'I've seen the way he holds you. Keep it up, and you'll regret it.'"

Piper swung her gaze to Chloe, who stared wide-eyed at Jake. Just what had been going on that her cousin wasn't telling her? The instant they were alone, Piper planned on drilling Chloe for information.

"We're getting out of here." Jake's tone said arguing would get them nowhere.

Piper's heart broke for Chloe.

"Wait. I can't skip this concert." Obviously Chloe

hadn't registered the tone as she leaned forward, gripping her hand around Jake's seat.

"We can fly you back in for the concert, bring more protection with us, but we need to get you to the ranch where this guy can't get to you." Jake turned at the sign that pointed to the airport.

"What about all our stuff? I have appearances scheduled this week. All that information is at the house." With each item listed, Chloe's voice grew more frantic.

Piper knew what needed done. Did she have the courage to do it?

"Chlo, this guy isn't playing games." Rafe turned in the seat.

Piper swallowed the heavy stone in her throat. "What if I go back to the house and gather up our stuff?" She hated how her voice came out soft instead of strong. "I can start calling our contacts and figuring out what we can do virtually from the ranch."

Chloe shook her head and gripped Piper's hand. "Piper, no—"

"Listen. It makes sense. I'm your manager. It's my job to take care of things." Piper interrupted before she lost her nerve and hugged Chloe close. "Rafe and I will gather everything up here, then drive down to this ranch of theirs."

"But what if he follows you guys, or what if he gets mad and hurts you?"

"Don't worry. We'll be quick, and Rafe will keep me safe." Piper gazed at Rafe, knowing he'd give his life so she wouldn't be harmed.

Rafe swallowed as he nodded. "Always."

Piper stared at him, trying to understand the shift in his expression. Did he feel the electricity zinging between them, or had her brain finally decided make-believe land was a better place to stay? He blinked and looked at Chloe. Yep, definitely all just in her head.

Rafe placed his hand on Chloe's knee. "Chloe, this will work. I can spot a tail a mile away. We'll take back roads and be at the ranch later tonight." His voice deepened. "I won't let anything happen to our Piper, I promise."

Everything faded as Piper's mind grabbed on to his "our Piper" comment. The two words shouldn't make her hair stand on end, but they did. If she thought about it, the words solidified their friendship in the same pattern as the past, the way he and Davis let her and Chloe tag along like lost little puppies. Yet something in his tone as he said it had her analyzing it from every angle, replaying the words in her mind.

Obsessing over Rafe's words was probably her mind's way of protecting her from their current frightening situation. Next thing she knew, they'd stopped and a frigid blast of air startled her from her thoughts. Chloe took out her phone and made a phone call. When she said Chet's name, Piper cringed. She should've thought about calling the band and letting them know what was happening. Great manager she turned out to be.

Chloe winced and peeked at Piper. Piper wondered just what Chet had said.

"Yeah, I have some interviews and stuff she's going to try to coordinate from Glenwood. Plus, her brother would flip if we left her here alone." Chloe shrugged and smiled at Piper.

Great, now Chet would also think of her as a child. Piper elbowed Chloe in the side and stuck out her tongue.

Chloe rolled her eyes. "Listen, Chet, I gotta go. Could you let the others know that we'll call later to work out Friday?" Chloe tapped the end icon and smiled at Piper in a way that made her stomach drop. "It seems your admirer is upset you're leaving town."

Piper groaned and rolled her eyes, guilt coating the back of her tongue. "I feel bad. Maybe I should've said yes."

"What's this?" Rafe turned in the seat and looked between the two of them.

Chloe had that look on her face that meant trouble. "My guitarist, Chet, has been wanting Piper to go out to dinner. She's sparked his fancy, some would say."

"You told him no?" Rafe's eyes narrowed at Piper, and his voice had that big brother tone to it.

"Yeah, but I keep wondering if I should just bite the bullet and go. We've spent a fair amount of time with him lately working on songs and such." Piper shrugged, not knowing why she told him all of this. "He's nice."

"But you're not attracted to him?" Rafe's question made her uncomfortable.

Why did it matter if she was attracted or not? It changed nothing. She was still her, and his interest wouldn't last. But how could she say that out loud?

"It's not that." Piper rubbed her collar, cursing her cheeks as they grew warm.

"So, you are attracted?" He pushed.

"He's hot." Chloe smiled and nudged Piper, dropping her throat into her stomach. "Smoking hot."

Rafe's muscles tightened. "Why not go out with him then?"

Her cheeks went from warm to white-hot, and the stress and fear pushed words past her ability to filter. "Because I'm not going to get attached to someone who will see the light sooner rather than later, especially with the amount of gorgeous groupies always storming him at the shows."

Why had she just said all that? She needed to go, get away from his scrutiny.

Rafe growled. "What is that supposed to mean?"

Piper crossed her arms and looked out the window, hoping to shut down this embarrassing conversation. "I'm done talking about this."

"Piper." The vehicle door opening broke off Rafe's words as Jake handed Chloe snow gear before going to check more things on the plane.

Piper took the opportunity to escape, opening her door to the freezing winter air. She didn't get any satisfaction as she slammed the door closed behind her. She stomped around the SUV and leaned against its side. She hated that she acted like an emotional teenager. Hated that everything was overwhelming her to the point of imploding.

She closed her eyes and let the cold air whipping her face slap her back to reality. Chloe needed her to be strong, needed her to focus and take care of things. Chloe would never leave if she worried about Piper. Piper pushed back her shoulders and prepared to give her best smile as she pushed Chloe into the plane.

"We need to go." Jake stalked to the SUV.

Piper threw her arms around Chloe's neck before her emotions broke through her facade. "I'll see you soon."

"Don't you think you should come with?" Chloe hadn't shown such hesitancy since she was first admitted into the hospital all those years ago.

"No, I need that information from the house." Piper squeezed Chloe and stepped back, nodding in confidence. She pushed her mouth into a smile. "Besides, we'll be right behind you. I say ice cream and chick flicks tonight."

Chloe laughed, the tension easing from her. "That sounds perfect."

Piper's heart thudded in her chest as she glanced at the dark clouds forming at the top of the mountain. She turned her gaze back to the plane, dropping her wringing hands to her side. Chloe would be all right, and when Piper and Rafe got to Glenwood, Piper would have a plan to not only distract Chloe from not being in Steamboat, but to keep the momentum of Chloe's career moving forward.

Rafe's arm settled across her shoulder as he waved at the airplane. "Come on. Let's get going."

She let him lead her around the front of the SUV, but couldn't help taking one last look at the small airplane. "Will they be all right?" Her eyes widened at the storm rolling in, and she grabbed his arm. "That storm looks bad."

Rafe lifted his hand and tucked a strand of hair that

had fallen from her braid behind her ear. "Jake is the best pilot I know. He wouldn't fly if he didn't think he could."

She nodded, and he leaned over and kissed her on the forehead like a child before guiding her into the front seat. Oh, dear Lord in heaven. If Rafe kept acting all sweet, she wouldn't be able to keep her heart in check. Maybe driving to Glenwood with just him wasn't such a great idea after all.

FIVE

"PIPER, ARE YOU READY YET?" Rafe surveyed the living room again, making sure they left nothing behind.

It hadn't taken Piper and him long to pack up and load the SUV. He'd rushed around helping carry heavy suitcases like some whipped puppy. She'd even looked at him strangely once, like maybe he'd grown two heads or something, and he had to shake his brains loose so he didn't make a complete fool of himself.

Why had Chloe said what she had in the car after Piper had gotten out? Chloe saying, "But she's still hung up on her first love. Too bad the idiot never saw her as anything but his friend's little sister," kept playing on auto-repeat in his head. Now he'd spent the last forty-five minutes thinking about the past and if Piper had ever shown any sign she liked him how Chloe said.

He groaned. "Knock it off, Malone."

"Everything okay?" Piper's question heated his neck with embarrassment that she had heard.

He peered up the staircase to give some smart-aleck

remark, but almost choked on his tongue instead. She looked stunning, though she wore a simple sweater and leggings. Her smile at him as she trailed her hand along the bannister had his heart thumping in his throat. Her long legs stepped gracefully from one stair to another.

It was like those corny chick flick movies the girls had forced him and Davis to watch where the high school sports star watches his date and stumbles like an idiot. He and Davis had always made so much fun of that, saying that would never happen in real life. They were wrong. Piper reduced Rafe to a teenage boy who couldn't find his tongue. She laughed, and the sound tumbled like fresh water over boulders.

Reality slammed into him. Beyond the fact that she was Davis's sister, she was too good for Rafe. He gazed down to his hands that shook and shoved them into his coat pockets.

"I swear, you'd think Chloe had lived here for months with the way her stuff had exploded across her room." Piper held up a high-heeled shoe. "I found this behind the plant. I can't even imagine how it got there."

Rafe swallowed and nodded.

She cocked her head. "Are you sure you're okay? You look pale. Do you want to wait and rest or maybe I could drive?" She looked out the window at the snow that fell steadily.

"I'm fine." Rafe yanked her coat up from the back of the couch and held it open for her. "Let's get going."

She shrugged and stepped up to him as he helped her into her coat. Her perfume assaulted his senses with pheromones that made his fingers tingle. He'd have to tell her to stop wearing it so he could concentrate. Wouldn't that be an awkward conversation? *Hey Pip, think you can stop wearing that perfume? It's making me crazy with thoughts of snatching you into my arms and kissing you senseless.*

His hands stilled on her shoulders. Kiss her senseless? His heart stuttered, then took off like a jackrabbit. He snatched his hands away and stepped back.

She turned her head and cocked it to the side. "Are you sure you're feeling okay? Maybe we should wait and leave tomorrow."

"I'm fine. Just ready to get out of here." He stalked past her to the garage. "Everything's locked up, so let's scoot."

"Okay, but if you start to not feel good, let me know. I can drive."

Great. Now she thought he couldn't drive? *Snap out of it, Malone. This is Davis's sister and one of your best friends growing up. Stop making things weird.*

By the time he had the car pulled out of the driveway and headed through town, he'd talked himself back to normalcy. At least, he hoped. Maybe she'd refrain from doing something sexy that would draw his mind back to the freak-out zone. Not likely, since his stupid brain had decided everything she did was hot. He clenched his hands on the steering wheel. *Stupid Chloe and her troubling suggestions.*

"Let's grab dinner. There won't be any places to stop once we leave town." Rafe clicked on his blinker and pulled into Dairy Queen. "I need a burger and you deserve chicken strips with an Oreo Blizzard."

She tipped her head back and laughed. "I can't believe you remember that."

He glanced over at her. Her cheeks and ears had pinked with a blush and her lips had parted as they pushed into a smile. She touched the collar of her sweater, drawing his gaze to her slender neck and long fingers. He tore his eyes away. Nope. She wasn't going to make it easy on him.

He shrugged, trying to be nonchalant. "Pipster, do you think I could forget all that money I forked out so you could have your weekly reward for doing well in geometry?"

She snorted. "As if. I bought dinner each week to pay you for your tutoring, Rooster."

Her use of his old nickname reminded him of all that they'd shared those years before he had followed Davis into the Army. If he could just keep all that past at the front of his brain, he could keep his focus off of how she'd changed. He pulled into the drive-thru and surveyed the menu.

"All right. Flamethrower combo and a large peanut butter shake for me. Chicken strips for you?" He turned to Piper.

She wrung her hands as indecision played across her face. "I should be safe and get a salad."

"What do you mean 'be safe'?"

She shrugged. "The chicken strips have so much gluten."

"So? Chloe's not here."

"I know. It's just I try to stay gluten-free, and I already bailed once on this trip."

"You're saying you've changed your entire lifestyle just because Chloe has to? Even when she's not around." Rafe couldn't believe what he was hearing. "I understand wanting to be healthy, but it's also good to cheat now and then. Don't you want the chicken strips?"

"Well ... yeah, but I want to support her, and scarfing down a bunch of stuff she can't eat doesn't make it any easier on her." Piper crossed her arms.

"But she's not here. She'll never know."

"But I will."

He stared at her a moment as her words processed. How much had she given up to take care of Chloe? Instances from their childhood came flooding back. How much had she always done to take care of everyone else?

His eyes narrowed. "You're getting the chicken fingers."

He rolled down the window and placed the order. He ignored her sputtering and huffing behind him. When he pulled his head back into the SUV and rolled up the window, she jabbed him in the arm.

"Ow, Pipstick, go easy."

She poked him again. "What if I wanted a salad?"

"Did you?" He lifted his eyebrow in a challenge.

"Not really." She waved her arm. "Still, I'm never going to eat all that food."

"So? I'll finish what you don't eat."

"Right. The human garbage disposal." She shook her head. "I'm surprised you're not fat with the way you eat."

"This is all muscle, sweetheart." He motioned up and down his body.

Her eyes followed, and she visibly swallowed. His

belly warmed at her perusal. What did she think when she looked at him?

"Meh." She lifted her shoulders and turned her attention out the windshield.

What? Rafe would've deflated like a popped balloon, but her neck and ears turned bright red. *Hmm. Interesting.* A smile bloomed across his face as he turned to pay the cashier.

Five minutes later, he'd scarfed down his burger, and they were on the highway headed out of town. Piper made little noises of appreciation that kept pulling Rafe's attention away from the road to her. Her eyes rolled into her head as she took her first bite of her Blizzard. She moaned and Rafe yanked his gaze back to the road.

"Wow, I forgot how good this is." She took another bite.

Rafe's eyes followed the lift of the spoon to her mouth. She licked her lips of the ice cream that stuck there. What would it be like to kiss those lips? Rafe swallowed and forced his gaze to stay on the road. Her kisses would probably be sweet, just like her.

"Maybe you should have them more often?" If he could just get her talking, he could get his mind out of places it shouldn't wander.

She laughed. "No, I definitely shouldn't. Not if I don't want to look like I did in high school."

"What do you mean? You looked fine in high school."

"You were gone in high school, remember?" She pointed a fry at him.

"Yeah, but I came back to visit, and Davis kept me updated with pictures."

"Nope, meals like these need to be limited to rare occasions. I never want to give anyone reason to call me a Wookiee again." Piper cleared her throat. "Besides, I enjoy eating healthier. I like the way I feel when I do. Most of the time, I don't even miss gluten."

"What do you mean, Wookiee? When did anyone call you that?"

"Are you kidding me? How about since junior high? It became a favorite in high school among the jock guys." Piper sighed. "I really don't miss those years at all."

"Why would they call you that? You looked nothing like that." Rafe gripped the steering wheel. How had he never known?

"It started when I shot up in eighth grade and towered over all the preppy girls. Add that I didn't get my hair under control until my junior year in high school, and I guess I made an easy target." She ran her hand through her hair, pulling it over her shoulder. "It wouldn't have been so bad if it had just been the girls, but our freshman year, the boys started making Wookiee sounds when I walked past in the hall. That kind of made things embarrassing."

"Why didn't you tell me?"

"What would that have done? It just would've made things worse."

She crunched into her chicken strip. The pause in the conversation filled the space in the SUV with tension. He hated that people had made her fun of in high school. She was right, though. Anything he would've said or done would've just backfired.

"I'm sorry, Piper."

Could the apology of one man make up for years of torment? He shook his head. Probably not.

"It's okay. You weren't ever like that."

"They were all idiots." Rafe scoffed. "You're a knockout. They all should have been scrambling to win your attention."

Now, why had he just said that? He rubbed the back of his neck with his hand and forced his eyes to stay forward. He felt her eyes on him, though, and the heat of her stare pulled his gaze to hers.

"I'm not a knockout." Her strained whisper just about broke his heart.

"Yeah, Piper, yeah you are. You make it hard for a man to focus." His voice felt stuck in his throat.

A gust of wind blew hard against the side of the SUV and yanked Rafe's attention back to the road. The storm had settled in, making driving hazardous, just like the swirl of his new realizations pounding against his thoughts. He should've sent her on the plane with Jake and gathered up all their stuff himself. With the way the snow blocked out his vision, the two-hour drive would take double that, at least. Now, he'd dropped that bomb of truth out into the open with no foxhole to jump in for safety. He didn't think he could joke his way out of this.

SIX

PIPER CLUNG to the door as the vehicle swerved on a patch of slick road. The snow fell so thickly she didn't know how Rafe could drive. Between the horrible road conditions and his words about her making it hard to think, her stomach had been in knots the last four hours of the drive. The wind hit the side of the car, and she slammed her eyes closed. She didn't want them open when the car careened off the edge of the road.

"Are you sure we shouldn't stop somewhere and wait this out?" Piper squeaked as the wind pushed them again.

"Once we get through the canyon, we'll be in Glenwood." Rafe's jaw clenched in the dim light from the dash. "I'd rather keep going until I get you safely home to the ranch."

She'd tried to keep the conversation flowing for the last four hours, hoping to keep herself from worrying over the weather and Chloe, but also to keep the exchange from straying into the uncomfortable again. Why she had ever thought it'd be a good idea to bring up her high school torture was beyond her. She would have preferred him never knowing that little bit of humiliating history.

Of course, then he never would have called her a knockout.

She peeked at him again, wondering if he'd spoken the truth.

The SUV swerved, and she blurted the first question that popped in her head to distract herself. "So you live at a ranch with a bunch of guys, what, like a special ops frat house or something?"

"We call it the MAN-sion. It's dreamy. You'll like it." He winked at her before turning his attention back to the road.

She rolled her eyes at his emphasis on man. "We call it or you call it? That sounds like something stupid you'd come up with."

"Hey, I resent that. I come up with great names. All the guys love it." Rafe's hidden smile ruined his hurt expression.

"Like your names for our fort growing up? Those weren't that great."

"I don't remember." Rafe's forehead scrunched as he leaned closer to the steering wheel.

"Two Dudes and Two Duds Place." Piper crossed her arms and leaned against the door, suddenly glad the trip had taken twice as long. It gave her the perfect opportunity to stare.

Rafe's head tipped back, and his full laugh filled the space. The sound swirled like hot cocoa down her throat and pooled in her belly. Gosh, she loved his laugh.

Her smile wavered. She would never recover from

this time with him. She'd spent half her life pining over Rafe, the boy. Age and life's trials had just made the boy into an even more incredible man that checked all her boxes and crossed all her t's in the love-of-your-life list. *Great. Old maidery, here I come.*

"Oh man, that was a great name." He wiped a tear from his eye.

"No, it wasn't."

"What did we end up naming it again? Probably something lame."

Piper cleared her throat. "The Shack."

Rafe started laughing again. "And that's better?" He hit the steering wheel with his hand. "We did have some transcendent moments out in that rickety thing, though I'm not sure if they'd be considered heavenly-inspired."

"How were we to know that book and movie would come out?" Piper turned forward. "And speak for yourself. That fort was my sanctuary. I spent hours talking to God out there."

The next few seconds felt pregnant, like the air grew thick and would pop.

"What kind of things did you talk about?" Rafe's low question had no laughter in it.

She shrugged, sorry she'd brought that up. Would everything she said lead her right into trouble?

"Stuff. Boy stuff." She pitched her voice like an elementary school kid taunting when she said boy, then twisted her hands in her sweater. "Silly stuff mostly, at first anyway. Then more serious as I got older." She sighed and leaned her head against the icy door window. "I spent hours there praying for you and Davis. Then hours praying for Chloe when she got so sick. Yeah, so, maybe the name fit after all."

She closed her eyes and willed down the burn of worry that lapped at her heart. It had become her constant companion over the years, but she resented its presence. She didn't want to be that person, the one always fretting over everything. It seemed since her parents' deaths, she couldn't avoid it no matter how much she ignored it. She tried so hard to hide her fretfulness, which made the heartburn worse.

Rafe's warm hand stilled hers that twisted in her lap. Her eyes popped open, and she peered at him. He gave her a soft smile and squeezed her hands.

"Thank you for your prayers, Piper. You don't know how much that means to me." He swallowed and turned his gaze back out the windshield.

She waited for him to pull his hand away, but he didn't. Instead, he pushed his hand between hers and threaded her fingers with his. Her chest expanded with so many emotions she couldn't catalog them properly. Joy, love, pain, and, yes, worry, all fluttered spastically against her heart.

His thumb started making slow circles on the back of her hand. She stared out the windshield, blinking to keep her tears firmly in her eye sockets. *Please stay put.* She didn't want to embarrass herself any more than she already had.

Something bounced in the splotch of light from the headlights.

"What the ..." Rafe's hand tightened in hers.

Another object pinged even closer.

"What is that?" Piper leaned forward to get a better look.

No sooner had the words escaped her mouth than a large rock the size of a football landed on the hood and rolled off the other side. Rafe jerked his hand out of hers as a crash hit the roof.

"Rockslide." His words tumbled fear into her throat.

He pushed on the gas and rocketed down the interstate, slipping this way and that. The pinging of rocks on metal barraged her ears. The road disappeared to rocks, dirt, and snow. They wouldn't make it.

Oh God, Lord, please. She didn't want to be buried alive.

The windshield splintered into a thousand spider webs before them. The baseball-sized rocks assaulting the vehicle thundered and pushed out all other sounds. Something large bounced into her door, pushing the car sideways and shattering glass across her.

"Piper, hold on." Rafe's yell barely reached her as her fear ripped screams from her soul.

She curled over her knees, trying to protect herself as rocks pelted her like hail through the busted window. She jerked as one hit behind her ear, exploding stars behind her eyelids. She was too tall—couldn't hide. She tried to cover her head better with her arms, tried to stifle her screams every time a rock struck.

Then, just as quickly as the onslaught began, the pummeling stopped, leaving wind and snow blowing through the busted window. She choked back a sob.

Don't fall apart now.

Another sob followed. She gritted her teeth against the heat of tears and pain coursing through her body.

"Piper, honey, hold on." Rafe soothed his hand across her back, and she flinched.

A whimper escaped. *Please, don't fall apart now.* The car slowed to a stop, and a click of a seatbelt being released sounded before Rafe's hand pushed her hair off her face.

"Oh, Pip, I'm so sorry." His voice sounded thick in her ears, and she wondered if they would ever work again.

She clenched her fingers in her hair. She wouldn't cry. Another sob choked her.

"Piper, where are you hurt?" He put pressure on her shoulder to lift her, but she shook her head. "Please, honey, let me see you."

His voice cracked, and her dam broke. Her shoulders shuddered as sob after sob tore from her chest. Rafe pulled her up, and she tucked her face into his neck. She fisted his shirt in her hands, trying desperately to control her emotions.

"Oh honey, please tell me you're okay." Rafe rubbed his hand on her back.

She flinched as pain shot across her skin. He groaned and leaned back, sliding the back of his fingers over her cheek. His muscles jumped under her hand pressed against his chest.

She swallowed down her pain and fear. "I'm okay." She forced out the words.

His breath came fast and choppy against her face. He

leaned his forehead against hers. His thumbs rubbed her cheeks.

"Phew. That was intense." His chuckle sounded forced.

She shuddered out a breath. "I was so scared."

He took three deep breaths before he spoke, tension building in the air around her. "Me too."

His breath touched her lips, almost like a kiss. The soft sensation uncurled the fist of fear in her stomach. All her daydreams didn't come close to the warmth that spread through her stomach and skated to her toes. She slid her hand up his chest and combed her fingers through his coarse beard.

She pushed her fingers along his jaw and cupped his head. "Rafe."

Everything she ever dreamed, all her hopes and fantasies, hovered a breath away. She didn't want to wonder anymore. Though her back and head throbbed, she was alive. She'd risk the plunge.

She kissed him, putting all her fear and yearning into the action. He responded with a moan and leaned closer, though the touch of his hands stayed gentle on her face. The warmth built to heat that threatened to singe her from the inside out. She needed air but was willing to drown if it meant dying while kissing Rafe.

A frigid blast of wind whipped through the broken window, causing her to gasp. He pushed back from her until he leaned against his door, his eyes wide upon his face and his chest heaving. Her lips tingled, and she brought her fingertips to them.

"That shouldn't have happened." Rafe's words tumbled her joy down like boulders in a landslide.

She turned to look out the windshield, her shoulders slumping. She refused to cry, refused to react, though his words had ripped her heart from her chest. He didn't know she'd spent years thinking about kissing him. That hours of her life were tied up into prayers for and dreams of him. She should've known the landslide created a moment of relief that expressed itself in a kiss. She should've known not to push it further in her head than it was.

"Piper." He leaned forward, but she put her hand up to stop him.

She couldn't hear his excuses now.

He cleared his throat. "I need to get the window covered and get on the road before we get stuck out here." His words conjured all kinds of images of them snuggling in the back of the SUV.

Maybe being stranded wouldn't be so bad after all. She snorted to herself. With the way he'd scrambled from her, trapped with him wouldn't include cuddling.

"Will the door open?" His question pulled her from her thoughts and made her cheeks warm.

She turned to the door, noticing for the first time how it had a slight bent toward her. Her hands slicked at the memory of the impact. She pushed the feeling aside and gripped the handle. The door didn't budge.

"No." She leaned her head out to see the damage, but the blowing snow and darkness obscured it.

Rafe placed his hand on her back, and she flinched at the pain. Her back had to look a mess.

"Can you crawl into the back seat? I'll get a trash bag and duct tape from the back to take care of the window, then I'll check out your back."

"Its fine, Rafe. I'll just have some bruises." She turned to him, the thought of him seeing her bare back making her sick to her stomach.

She couldn't handle throwing herself at him and showing her chub all in one day. His eyes narrowed. He made a noise in his throat before pushing his door open and marching to the back of the vehicle.

She climbed over the seat, wincing as she did. Yep, definitely going to be sore, but sore beat dead, any day.

She brushed off the glass on the seat, realizing that both hers and the back window had shattered. When Rafe climbed in the front, she helped him tape up the windows the best she could. With that finished and the snow no longer filling the floorboards, she turned to toss the tape and extra bags into the back.

Before she could protest, Rafe got into the back seat with her, the freezing wind and her anxiety skittering down her spine. He slammed the door, reached over the back of the seat to grab a first-aid bag, and glared at her.

"I'm checking your back." He used that tone he and her brother had perfected growing up, that I'm-taking-charge tone.

She crossed her arms over her chest. "I don't think so."

"It's me or the hospital."

"Over some bruises?"

He wouldn't.

"Piper, please." His voice cracked, and he jerked his

head to look out the windshield. He took a deep breath and peered back at her. "Please."

He cut his words off and looked at his hand clenched around the bag. His anguish loosened the humiliation that burned her insides. She eased her hand over his. She didn't want to hurt him, even if it would embarrass her.

She pulled her bulky sweater off, glad she'd worn the tank top underneath. She could do this. She swallowed and turned, pulling her hair over her shoulder. She closed her eyes as he gently pulled her hem up.

He hissed. "Oh, honey."

The sweet word eased her tension. "That bad?"

"Baby, you're going to look like a blackberry pie by tomorrow." He smoothed his fingers over her skin, spreading some kind of ointment over it.

"Hmm, your favorite." She tried to chuckle.

"My favorite, for sure." Rafe's audible swallow and odd tone made her wish she could see his face.

She closed her eyes, allowing her body to relax under his doctoring. His soft touch eased all the fear from the last hours and had her muscles relaxing. She rolled her head and pain spiked from behind her ear. Groaning, she gingerly lifted her hand to her head and felt a large bump.

"Here, let me check." Rafe squeezed her fingers and parted her hair. "Pip, you took the brunt of the attack, that's for sure."

"I think maybe the car got the brunt." She flinched and hissed as he gently probed her wound. "I just got the leftovers."

"That was a lot of leftovers." He sighed and

smoothed her hair down. "The only spot I think you didn't get hit is right here."

His voice dipped low as his fingers skimmed a section on her left shoulder. She froze as her skin sparked alive, heating where he touched and raising goosebumps where he didn't. She squeezed her sweater in her hands.

"Piper, I know you don't want to, but I need to take you to the hospital to make sure you don't have any internal bleeding or broken bones." He pulled her shirt hem down, careful not to touch her back.

"Over some bruises?"

"You're not seeing what I'm looking at. It's more than just a few bruises."

"Is it necessary?"

"Yeah." He sighed. "Let's get going, Pipstick."

She turned to see what his expression would tell her and spied the busted windshield. "Will you even be able to see the road?"

Her voice came out breathy, like she'd just run a marathon. She'd never run for fun a day in her life, but the way her heart and lungs seemed bottled up and confined in her chest, she imagined she'd feel like this if she did. He sat close, so close his breath skated across her shoulder.

"Yeah, I can drive." He hadn't checked the windshield. "I can't stay here."

His gaze glued to her lips as he leaned forward. She definitely wanted to stay and find out what being trapped in a snowstorm with Rafe would be like. She angled closer. He jerked and gave a slight shake of his head.

"I mean, we can't stay here." He swallowed hard, his Adam's apple bobbing.

"Why not?" She wanted to stay in this vehicle with a desperation that rivaled any desire she'd ever had.

"Why not?" Rafe repeated her question like he couldn't remember what they were talking about.

She liked this side of Rafe she'd never seen before. The one where he was flustered and fumbled with his thoughts and words. Could she really cause his bewilderment? She chewed on her bottom lip, and his eyebrows furrowed like she confused him. She licked her lips, and his eyes widened. Discovering this Rafe proved too much fun. Now, she just needed to convince him staying put would be the safest route.

SEVEN

WHAT ARE YOU DOING, Malone?

Rafe had asked himself that question repeatedly over the last half hour as he'd scrambled back into the driver's seat, picked his way through the Glenwood Canyon, and drove to the hospital. He kept his eyes glued to the road beyond the busted windshield, not because it required his complete attention, which it did, but because if he even chanced one peek at Piper he'd pull the vehicle over and answer the expectation he'd heard in her wispy voice— quell the disappointment that had widened her eyes when he'd fumbled out of the backseat.

He clenched his jaw. For Pete's sake, he'd run like a chicken from a fox. That was the problem. She was foxy as all get out, and she didn't even know it. She called to him like a siren with her tender heart and big brown eyes. He couldn't answer the call, though. She was too pure for him, and he couldn't cross that line against Davis.

His thoughts stalled as he pulled out of the hospital parking lot after making sure Piper hadn't busted anything. Why couldn't he cross that line? They were all adults now. He wouldn't use or hurt her, and he and Davis had gone through enough that their friendship wouldn't be compromised. Besides, Davis still spent most of his time on overseas missions. He wouldn't even know until Rafe put a ring on Piper's finger and a wedding date got set.

He almost swerved into the other lane. When had he jumped from kissing Piper to marrying her? He couldn't help peeking at her in the rearview mirror. She'd pulled her hair over her right shoulder, and Rafe imagined the soft skin hidden under her sweater. He'd made a dire mistake kissing her back. One taste had infused her into his soul, making him long to drink from her well forever.

Man, he needed to rein in his thoughts before he went all poet on her and started spouting sonnets. The facts still hadn't changed. She was Davis's sister. Rafe didn't deserve her. Period. She groaned and shifted in her seat.

"Honey, we're almost there." He cringed. He had to stop calling her that, but it seemed to keep slipping out on its own.

"Good. I'm getting a little sore now." Her laugh sounded forced. "I don't think sitting so long has helped. How long until the pain killers the hospital gave me kick in?"

She had to be more than a little sore. He bet her every breath pained at the moment with the deep bruises she'd sustained. His forehead creased. Did she always downplay her hurt like that?

"Shouldn't be long now. I think we should end this

night with some cookies or ice cream or something to reward ourselves for making it."

She shifted in the seat. "Actually, I think a hot mug of tea sounds good." She shifted again. "And sleep. Lots and lots of sleep."

He could think of other rewards, but he wouldn't bring those up. He glanced at her. The side of her head rested on the seat, and her eyelashes lay against her cheeks. His heart double timed it in his chest. Man, she was so beautiful. The men where she lived must be idiots. Who was he kidding? He was an idiot for never seeing it.

He gritted his teeth and focused on driving the last few miles to the ranch. When they got home, he'd have to keep his distance. With them being at the ranch, he could bury himself in work and not screw things up more than he already had. His heart felt strangled in his chest. He didn't want to hide away from her.

"We're here." His voice croaked as he pulled up to the gate and punched in the code.

Her small gasp pulled his lips into a smile. "Rafe, what is this place?"

"Silver Wolf Ranch." He drove down the drive through the trees. "My friend Zeke bought this and started Stryker Security. It's pretty insane, all fancy-shmanchy. It works for us, though."

"You live here?" She leaned forward between the seats and moved her body around to try to peer out the busted windshield.

"Yep." He pointed down the road that broke off from the main driveway. "My place is that house down that road. This house here is where Zeke and his family live and where our clients stay when they need sheltering."

"Both these houses are enormous. Why would anyone need two houses this big on one property?"

"I think originally it was some kind of guest ranch where people vacationed." Rafe shrugged and he pulled to a stop. "Works for us though."

"Will you give me a tour while we're here?" She winced as she turned her head his way.

What was he doing, sitting out here in the cold? He needed to get her inside and get her settled. He turned off the car and opened the door.

"Sorry, honey, but it's a long walk up to the front door."

"It's okay." She smiled up at him weakly. "I've been bolstering myself since we left the hospital, telling myself not to be a wuss."

"You've never been a wuss. You were always right there with us in the thick of things growing up."

She groaned as she moved her legs out the door. "That's because I didn't want to be left behind."

He helped her out of the vehicle, her words pinging through his head. She had gone along with their antics because she didn't want to be left behind? She laid her forehead on his collarbone, her stuttering breath blowing hot air down his shirt. He loved that her height kept him from bending over. He liked that neither of them had to be uncomfortable when they held each other.

"I wanted to be baking and reading, but I didn't want to be alone. I always had fun, though, so ..." She shrugged, took a deep breath, and huffed it out. "Wow. That hurt."

"Let's get inside." Rafe kissed her on the forehead and pulled away.

She grabbed the open flaps of his coat. "Thank you for getting us here safe."

"What happened?" Zeke's barked question startled them apart.

Piper winced, and Rafe slid his arm around her waist to lead her inside. Zeke rushed down the steps, skidding to a halt as his gaze took in the vehicle. His eyebrows flew to his hairline.

Rafe glanced over his shoulder and almost stumbled. The entire side of the SUV looked like a semi had hit it. It was a miracle Piper wasn't hurt more than she was. He shook off the lightheadedness that came with that realization and continued up the stairs to the front door.

"Rockslide." He clapped Zeke on the shoulder as he passed. "Almost spent the night in a pile of rubble."

Piper whimpered, then cleared her throat. Why did she think she had to hide her discomfort from him? From her comment, it sounded like she hid a lot from all of them. He didn't like that thought.

"Are you guys okay?" Zeke asked as he followed them to the house.

"Mostly. Piper took a beating on her back when the rocks decided they wanted to be in the car rather than out." He brought Piper over to the kitchen island and placed her on a stool. "Zeke, I'd like to introduce you to Piper Fields."

Piper gave a small smile, though her face was pale and pinched. "We met a few years back when I came to see Davis."

"I remember." Zeke pushed his lips up into that smile that made women swoon at his feet.

If Zeke wasn't happily married, Rafe would've decked him. He shook his head. Why was he so jealous?

Piper glanced around the room. "Did Chloe head to bed? What time is it anyway?"

She pulled up her sleeve to check her watch and winced.

"Maybe we should just get you upstairs so you can sleep." Rafe pushed her hair back behind her ear, and she leaned her head into his touch.

Zeke cleared his throat, drawing Rafe's attention to Zeke's uncomfortable shifting. "We have a problem. Chloe and Jake didn't make it back."

Rafe was glad Jake had turned back to Steamboat. That storm had blown in much quicker than either of them expected. Piper stood up slowly, bracing herself against the stool.

"So are we sending a team up in the morning? I-70 will probably be closed with that slide, but we could get to Steamboat through Meeker." Rafe ran his hand across the back of his neck, exhaustion pulling at his shoulders.

Could he persuade Piper to stay here with him? He peeked at her. Doubt it. Concern had replaced the pain written across her face.

Zeke shook his head. "They didn't turn back. ATC received a mayday call. They had to do an emergency landing."

Piper's hand grabbed Rafe's coat flap. "What do you mean? Like at another airport?"

Zeke's skin bunched around his eyes as he shook his head. "No. They put down in the mountains."

"Mayday, as in crashed?" Piper's voice rose, and she pulled on Rafe's coat.

Zeke nodded, and Piper's grip on Rafe's coat released. Her eyes grew wide with fear, and she buckled next to him. He led her to the couch so she could sit.

"Get her water," Rafe commanded Zeke, not taking his eyes off Piper's face. "What happened with Jake?"

"Not sure, but they both made it. ATC said the call came in with a location and two survivors." Zeke set the glass of water on the coffee table.

"Rafe?" Her voice broke as her eyes darted from him to Zeke as a single tear tracked down her cheek. "Chloe? Is she okay?"

"Yeah, Pip." He leaned forward and brushed the moisture away with his thumb. Zeke's eyes went wide in Rafe's peripheral, but he didn't care. "They're both fine. Jake called in their location and as soon as the storm passes, we can go get them."

She collapsed against him, burying her face in his neck. Her sobs caused a sharp pain in his heart. How much worry could one person hold before they crumbled? He'd take care of this, have everything planned so they could head out the minute the storm lifted. While they waited, he'd track down this guy that stalked Chloe so Piper wouldn't have to worry about that anymore either. Then when he finished that, he'd figure out what he'd do with the desires raging in his chest. Desires he shouldn't think about, like holding Piper close for the rest of his life.

EIGHT

PIPER'S EYES opened and skipped around the unfamiliar bedroom, trying to remember just where she and Chloe were now. She stretched and stifled the movement as pain ratcheted through her body. The night before, and the realization that Chloe was missing, hit Piper anew. She needed to get up, see what she could do to help.

She groaned as she rolled off the mattress. Her suitcase sat on the bench at the foot of her bed. Rafe must've brought it up last night after she'd fallen asleep. Her cheeks warmed in embarrassment at how she'd fallen apart. Goodness, she hadn't even been able to walk up the stairs. How Rafe had carried her giant self up here still shocked her. She placed her hands on her hot cheeks. How humiliating.

She reached into her suitcase and hissed with pain. She blew out a long breath. Maybe a hot shower would help ease the muscles. Ten minutes later, she stepped out of the shower, the pain not any less than it had been before. A knock on the door had her scrambling to wrap herself in the robe that hung in the bathroom.

"Piper, it's Sam, Zeke's wife. Rafe said you might need some help." A sweet voice came through the door, relaxing Piper's shoulders.

Tears pricked her eyes, and she blinked them away. Rafe's attentive care had made the panic of Chloe's crash not escalate too far. After bringing Piper upstairs, he'd lain with her while she bawled like a baby. She must have fallen asleep in the middle of her breakdown.

She couldn't do that again. She needed to be strong. Needed to be someone others could count on, not someone needing to be taken care of.

She put her pep talk to action and called through the pain as she reached into her suitcase for clothes. "Come in."

The door opened, and a beautiful woman with the kindest smile came in carrying a steaming mug. She wore a loose sweater over her long torso that accentuated her long legs. She had to be as tall as Piper, but somehow Sam pulled off looking like some kind of goddess. Why couldn't Piper have that slim grace instead of the lumbering form she did?

"Please tell me that's coffee?" Piper pushed her self-loathing down to smile back at the woman. It wasn't Sam's fault Piper's thoughts always brimmed with self-consciousness.

"It is, and I brought our secret bruise ointment with me." Sam's eyes twinkled. "Rafe's been pacing with worry over you. When he heard the shower running, he just about jumped out of his skin, then started commanding us all around."

Piper shook her head. Rafe wouldn't have done that over her. "You're exaggerating. He's probably just deep in a game on his phone or something and doesn't want to lose."

Sam shook her head, her black curls that had fallen out of her ponytail bouncing against her dark cheeks, and handed Piper the mug. "Rafe is not in Rafe-form this morning. You've somehow pushed all his boyish charm out to reveal a very bossy man."

Piper squeezed her hands around the mug, telling herself not to allow those words to go to her head. "I doubt that. He's just worried about Chloe and Jake." Piper cringed at her desperate tone and hurried on before Sam could say anything else. "What super-secret ointment do you have for me? Please tell me it'll heal my back, and I'll be good as new by tonight."

Sam laughed. "I wish it worked that fast. It's just an ointment Zeke's stepmom Jodi makes up. She's into essential oils and natural healing." Sam sighed. "She has all the guys using oil blends. It's funny, but the crazy stuff works."

Sam opened and sniffed the jar. She froze, her eyes winging wide as her dark skin turned a grayish tint. She pushed the ointment into Piper's hands and took off for the bathroom. When sounds of retching came from the other room, Piper set the ointment and coffee down and rushed after Sam.

Sam hunched over the toilet, and a sharp pain pinched Piper's chest at the woman's sickness. Piper grabbed a washcloth from the counter, ran cold water over it, and knelt next to Sam. Piper pushed Sam's loose curls out of her face and laid the cool cloth on her neck.

"Do you want me to go get Zeke?" Piper asked softly.

Sam's tiny shake of her head had Piper's shoulders relaxing. She didn't want to go out there until she had armored herself with the confidence her new wardrobe gave her instead of looking like a barbet dog wrapped in a tortilla. Guilt washed over her at the selfish thought. How could she worry about that right now when Sam was so sick?

Sam grabbed the washcloth from her neck and flopped against the glass shower stall. "I'm so sorry." She wiped her face and took a deep breath. "What a great way to greet company. Hey, nice to meet you, now I'm going to throw up in front of you."

"Think nothing of it. I'm just sorry you aren't feeling well. Are you sure you don't want me to go get Zeke?" Piper twisted her hands in the robe's tie.

"No, please. He'll just worry and make me go back to bed." Sam rolled her eyes, but her smile held a secret tenderness that made Piper's throat thick with envy. "Ever since we found out I'm pregnant last week, he's been impossible. Like lifting a pencil or walking down the stairs is suddenly too much for me."

The joyful news caused Piper's eyes to fill with moisture that she blinked away. "Congratulations. That's such exciting news." One she wondered if she'd ever get to share herself.

"It's still early in the pregnancy, so we aren't telling the guys yet." Sam groaned. "They're all so protective, I'll probably be rolled into bubble wrap for the next thirty-four weeks. Sosimo's wife, June, and I have talked about how we may have to disappear to Zeke's island when the protectiveness becomes stifling."

Piper swallowed at how wonderful that sounded. She hadn't felt that way since her parents' deaths. Sure, her brother and Rafe had protected her and Chloe growing up, but it hadn't been in a way that made her feel cherished. More like an annoying big brother way, which had broken her teenage heart on more than one occasion with her crush on Rafe.

Piper forced a laugh. "After last night's storm, an island escape sounds tempting."

"Last night's storm is still raging." Sam's soft whisper snapped Piper's stare up from where it had focused on the patterned tile floor.

She scrambled up, wincing at the sharp pain radiating across her back. Dashing to the window, she threw open the curtains. Snow whipped so thickly on the other side of the glass that Piper could barely see light from the windows of another building farther out. The window rattled and pinged as the storm assaulted it. How would Chloe be able to survive in this? Piper had to do something, anything, to try to help her.

She spun from the window and flew to her suitcase. She pulled out the first pair of leggings and sweater she found, hoping they looked half decent together and untied her robe.

"Let's get your back looked at." Sam's voice caused Piper to yelp and grab the edges of the robe before it fell to the floor. "Sorry. Didn't mean to frighten you."

Piper shook her head. "I just got tunnel vision and forgot you were here. Sorry." She gathered her clothes, getting ready to change in the bathroom now that Sam wasn't there anymore. "Don't worry about my back. I don't want to make you sick again. It'll be okay after I get something in my stomach and take some painkillers."

"Oh, no. Rafe will kill me if I don't get this stuff on you. I'm fine now. It's usually just the first scent that does it to me."

"Rafe won't care—"

Sam's snort interrupted Piper. "Rafe cares. Cares a lot by the way he's acting."

"No, I mean, yes, he does care, always has, but it's like a big brother care." Though the way he'd kissed her last night wasn't a brotherly kiss.

Of course, after the kiss, he had gone back to his let's-look-after-Piper self from growing up. More than likely, he had returned her kiss because of the intensity of the moment, not because his thoughts toward her had changed. *That shouldn't have happened.* His words slammed back into her mind. He was right. Kissing him had been a colossal mistake.

"Hmm. Is that how you see him?" Sam's guarded tone had Piper swallowing.

She didn't want to tell her new friend her deepest secret. Piper had spent half her life covering it up. She could get through a few hours being stuck here until the storm passed and they could get to the plane crash, pretending like her heart hadn't firmly wrapped itself around Rafe.

"That's what I thought." Sam smirked.

"Wait, what? I didn't say anything."

"You didn't have to. You're in love with him. It's written all over your face."

Piper collapsed onto her bed, squeezed her eyes shut, and buried her face in her hands. "No, no, no. I can't ... he doesn't." How had her world crumbled so fast? "He can't find out."

"Why?"

"Because I'll never be anything more than just Davis's little sister to Rafe," Piper muttered through her hands.

"From what I've seen, and what Zeke told me about last night, Rafe isn't thinking you're his little sister. Far from it." Sam turned her finger at Piper. "Now turn around and let me get this stuff on your back before Rafe barges up here in a frantic huff."

Piper turned around and lowered the robe in a daze over what Sam had just said. The possibility of Rafe finally noticing her still seemed slim, especially after his comment when she'd kissed him. It didn't matter to her heart though. It beat like hummingbird wings at the prospect.

Sam sucked in a sharp breath, steering Piper's mind from its crash course. "Oh, Piper."

"It's okay. It could be a lot worse." Piper flinched at Sam's soft touch on her skin. "We could've been buried alive in the landslide."

"As long as rescue came, that might not have been a bad thing." Sam chuckled. "I know I wouldn't mind being trapped with Zeke."

Piper sighed and closed her eyes as she tried to stay

relaxed and not jerk with each painful touch. "Yeah. I guess that wouldn't have been so bad."

She told her brain not to think about what could've happened in the dark confines of the SUV. It didn't listen. In fact, it brought up all kinds of memories from the day before that just fueled her minimally subdued attraction into overdrive. If she didn't watch it, she'd tumble herself headlong into heartbreak again. This time, she didn't know if she would survive.

NINE

"HOW LONG DOES it take to put a little ointment on and get dressed?" Rafe paced in the kitchen and pushed his hand through his hair.

"Man, what's with you?" Zeke laughed as he scooped up another bite of cereal.

"What? Nothing. I'm just worried about her is all."

Rafe went to the coffeepot and poured himself another cup, though, from the way his body jittered, he'd drunk enough. Zeke didn't know that. So Rafe took a deep drink to distract his friend from asking questions.

"It's more than that." Zeke shook his head. "You're acting strange. Plus, you forget I saw the way you were with her last night. Davis is going to freak."

Rafe's shoulders slumped as he turned to face Zeke and leaned against the counter. Zeke was right. Rafe felt much more than just worry over Piper. The coffee soured in his stomach, and he clunked the mug on the counter.

With the way she worried, did Piper live with this burn in her stomach all the time? How had she not bit all her nails to nothing and have dark circles the size of silver dollars under her eyes?

He rubbed a hand down his tired face. He hadn't slept a wink. He'd lain with Piper well after she'd fallen asleep, just watching her while he ran his fingers through her silky hair. When he'd finally pulled himself away, he hadn't made it far.

He'd have to talk to Zeke about purchasing a more comfortable couch in the sitting room upstairs. Rafe shook his head. He could've just slept in one of the other bedrooms. There were plenty in the upstairs of the main house they used when clients needed a safe place to stay. A chuckle drew Rafe's attention across the kitchen.

"What's so funny?" Rafe forced himself to relax his shoulders as he looked at Zeke.

"You, dude." Zeke shook his head, a smile stretched wide across his face. "So have you always loved her or is this a new development?"

Rafe straightened, his heartbeat picking up. "I don't—"

"I'm not Davis. You can tell me."

Rafe shifted his feet and picked up the coffee to keep his hands still. What could he say? That he couldn't stop thinking about her? That he hadn't wanted to leave her last night and had spent a bulk of the night wondering what it would be like to hold her tight for the rest of his life? Or how about that his heart finally felt sparked to life after two years of feeling frozen with shame? He couldn't do anything about it, though. He couldn't taint her—couldn't ruin her innocence.

"It doesn't matter. Nothing can come of it." Rafe picked up the coffee mug and took a drink.

"Why not?"

"It's not Davis, well, partly." Rafe cringed at what Davis would do. "He'd probably kill me, which would be for the best. I don't deserve her, not after what I've done."

Zeke's eyebrows slammed low over his eyes. "What do you mean by that?"

"Come on, man. You know what I did that last mission. You know how I took that kid's life. My soul has a black mark that can never be wiped clean. How can I possibly consider a relationship, especially with someone as innocent and pure as Piper, when that shame saturates me?" Rafe slammed the mug down and turned to slink into his office downstairs.

Zeke blocked Rafe's escape, his arms crossed over his chest. "You did what any of us would've done, Rafe. It was war. You weren't the one who made that kid a soldier."

"No, but I was the one who took his life."

Zeke muttered a curse. "You didn't. The ones who put the gun in that kid's hands did."

Rafe shook his head and tried to get past, but Zeke stopped him with a hand on Rafe's chest. His eyes burned hot, and he panicked that he'd start blubbering like a baby. He turned his head to the side and blinked to clear his emotions.

"Zeke, I could've neutralized him, could've used non-lethal force."

"No, you couldn't have. Not if we didn't want the entire mission to blow up in our faces."

"It did anyway."

"But not because of you," Zeke whispered.

Oh, shoot. Here comes the waterworks. Rafe sniffed.

"We've all had to do stuff that haunts us in the night. It's an occupational hazard." Zeke clapped Rafe on the shoulder. "If there's something between you and Piper, go for it. We all deserve happiness after all that we've sacrificed."

Female talking drew both their eyes to the stairs. Sam leaned over and whispered something to Piper that made her smile. The smile didn't push the tension from Piper's shoulders, though.

"Just do me a favor." Zeke stepped next to Rafe so he could face the women.

"What's that?"

Zeke nudged Rafe and lowered his voice. "Let me be there when you tell Davis. That's going to be a show I don't want to miss."

Rafe snorted. "No way. I think I'll just steal her away where it's only the two of us."

That idea burned hot in his stomach as his gaze connected to hers. The tension in her shoulders relaxed, causing the burn to spread like wildfire through his veins. He wanted to ease her worry, help her with the load she carried on her shoulders. He wanted to discover what Piper wanted out of life—not for Chloe or Davis or himself—but what dreams Piper had buried beneath her support of others.

She walked to him, her hands wringing in front of her. "What can I do to help get ready for when the storm passes?"

Here he wanted to take her worry away and right off the bat he would have to pile more on. "Pip, the storm isn't supposed to pass for a few days."

"No, Rafe, but Chloe—"

"Will be safe with Jake," he interrupted, balling his hands so he didn't reach out and grab her. "We keep the plane stocked with enough provisions to get two people through a week or more."

She shook her head, her eyes wide with fear. How had he never noticed the flecks of gold in the brown?

"But—"

"I promise, they'll be fine." He couldn't resist and lifted his hand to push the wet curls from her face that had escaped the messy bun she'd pulled it into.

She grabbed onto his arm. "Would you listen? I need to see the provisions they have."

"They're basic MREs. Nothing fancy."

She stomped her foot and threw up her hands. The action was adorable and so out of character for the sweet, mild Piper. She poked his chest.

"Rafe Marcus Malone, go get those MREs, or whatever they are, right now."

Rafe rubbed where she'd poked. "Tone it down, Bossy Pants."

Her gaze speared him as she grabbed his arm. "Please. I need to know."

"Why? It won't change anything."

She shook her head and blinked. "I need to know so we can see just how bad it'll be when we find them." She swallowed hard. "I need to know that she's not starving."

Her voice cracked, and he pulled her into his arms.

He rubbed her back but jerked his hand away when she flinched. He groaned, not knowing where to touch her that wouldn't hurt. He settled with rubbing his hands down her arms and twining his fingers between hers.

"Okay, I'll go grab the packs from the garage. Why don't you have a seat, and I'll make you something to eat while you look them over?"

Relief shined from her face, and Rafe barely stopped himself from kissing her to ease the rest of the worry away. Instead, he led her to the stools at the kitchen island, brought her a mug of coffee, and rushed to the garage where they kept a cabinet full of supplies. He grabbed as many as he could hold, then hurried back into the kitchen.

"I don't know which ones they have, but you can get an idea from these." He dumped the packets on the counter in front of Piper and moved to start breakfast.

She grabbed his arm and stood. "Thank you, Rafe." She sighed and leaned closer. "My mind is going nuts right now. Probably would be a blubbering pile of mess, but, with you here, I'm not so scared." She gazed at him with bright eyes. "I'm so glad you're here with me. I don't think I could handle this without you."

Purpose fluttered in his chest. He swallowed to loosen the boulders that had lodged in his throat, but they wouldn't budge. He gave a quick nod, squeezed her hand, sending shock waves up his arm, and distanced himself under the guise of making her breakfast so he could think straight.

Maybe Zeke was right. Maybe Rafe could put the past behind him and let his feelings for Piper grow. He was tired of pretending everything was okay. Tired of constantly joking to cover his sins. He wanted the joy to be real, not just a front. Maybe in supporting the most giving person he'd ever known, he could tip the balance and cleanse himself of the darkness that had tangled in his soul.

TEN

RAFE GROWLED AT HIS SCREEN, pushing back from his desk and digging his hands into his hair. It shouldn't be this hard to track down one stalker. Whoever this guy was, he'd hidden his tracks so well no amount of digging could root him out.

Or maybe the Piper distraction of the last two days was screwing with his normally genius computing abilities. He shook his head. What a mess.

Hooting laughter sounded from upstairs. He cringed. He should be up there with Piper and the others keeping Chloe's band members company, but his office had become his hideout.

After that first morning, he'd had to take a step back. The realization of all Piper could mean to him had him running scared. He didn't like the feeling—didn't like that he'd hid in his man cave like a frightened rabbit. He wasn't a fluffy bunny, for Pete's sake. He was a wolf or a mountain lion or some other fierce, powerful animal. He'd get himself all talked up, go search her out when the desire to be in her presence became too much to ignore, then find himself scurrying back down to his burrow when just a bump of an elbow, her laugh, or her silky voice would send shivers up and down his spine.

Stupid Zeke for putting insane thoughts in Rafe's head. He'd have to come up with an exceptional way to get back at the meddling man. One conversation and Rafe's world had turned on its head. Who was he kidding? One look at Piper and his world had spun off its axis.

Now she sat upstairs, entertaining the supposedly super-hot, insanely talented Chet and the other band members while Rafe hid ... again. He'd played nice for about two point three seconds when the band members had first arrived at the ranch. Greeted each of them with a smile and a handshake without breaking bones as he squeezed. But when Chet had lingered in his hug to Piper and whispered something that made her head duck and her cheeks pink, Rafe had booked it to his burrow before the jealousy that tinged his vision red erupted into, at best, strutting like a rooster and pecking the competition or, at worse, pummeling the man and throwing him out into the storm that still raged.

Why had Sam thought inviting the band members over for dinner would be a good idea? They didn't need to be entertained while waiting for news from Chloe. They were musicians. They could entertain themselves.

"Rafe?" Piper's sweet voice jerked his head to where she stood next to him.

How had she gotten this close without him knowing?

He straightened in his chair and rolled his shoulders. His mind had finally turned to mush.

"I didn't mean to scare you." She bit her bottom lip in concern, and all Rafe wanted to do was pull her to him and kiss the worrying action away.

"You didn't scare me."

Liar. She terrified him, but not in the way she thought.

She stepped closer, her perfume surrounding him and snapping his senses to alert. He took a deep breath through his nose, filling himself to the brim with the scent that lured him. His body trembled, and he wasn't sure if he was the rabbit shaking with panic or the wolf anticipating his pounce.

She ran a hand across his shoulders, causing his muscles to jump. *Well, great. Rabbit it is.*

"Rafe, why don't you come and join us?"

He shook his head. "Can't. Not until I figure out who this stalker is."

"You need a break. You look horrible." She chuckled as she ran her fingers through his hair to straighten it.

The touch stood all his hair on end and rushed heat from his scalp to his toes. He closed his eyes, savoring the feeling but also reining his crazy thoughts in, thoughts of locking the door and begging her to take a chance with him and forget the guitarist which bordered on plain dumb. She hadn't said a word about Chet since that day in Steamboat, and even her greeting when the dude had arrived hadn't been overly warm.

He cleared his throat. "I still have some trails I need to track down. Don't want to stop until I do."

She sighed. Her hand trembled in his hair before she pulled it away. His eyes popped open as her tension leaked into the space between them. He grabbed her hand as she brought it down to her side.

"What is it, Pipster?"

Piper shrugged and shook her head. "Nothing."

Her unease had the wolf in him tossing the rabbit aside. "Piper, please."

She lifted her free hand to rub her collar and rolled her eyes. "I'm just being stupid."

He squeezed her hand and growled, the very thought angering him. "No, you aren't. You're amazing, incredibly intelligent, and so beautiful."

Her eyes widened. Shoot. He hadn't meant to say that last part.

He cleared his throat and gave her fingers a little shake, hoping to skirt over his slip. "So, Pipstick, what's got you venturing into the Cave of Manly Awesomeness?"

She snorted and peered around the room, her shoulders relaxing. He wondered what she thought of the banks of computer screens all running different programs, the whiteboard wall where he scribbled thoughts and equations, and the Mario Kart figurines lined in a race along his desktop. Sweat broke out along his neck at her perusal.

"Is that what this is?" She smirked, drawing his gaze to her lips.

She pulled her hand out of his and reached for Princess Peach, twisting the toy in her hand as she leaned against his desk. She shrugged, and her shoulders rose with tension again. What had her so wound up?

"It's just that these guys are Chloe's friends. I'm usually just in the background, a glorified groupie who makes the snacks and gets them gigs."

"I thought you and Chet were friends at least. Hasn't he been trying to get you on a date?"

Her cheeks pinked, and Rafe wondered why she blushed.

"Agh, it's so awkward. He's nice, a really smart and great guy. Went to college for computers and uses it to make amazing music." She brought the toy up to her face, turning it this way and that. "But I just don't feel any attraction to him like that, which makes me feel guilty and like an idiot. What kind of woman wouldn't be falling at his feet?"

Rafe's head became light with her comment and made his tongue loose. "Why aren't you attracted to him?"

Her cheeks turned bright red as she peeked at him before gluing her eyes on the toy in her hand. "He's not really my type." She sighed and set the toy back in line. "What I want to do is just hide so I don't have to make small talk and pretend everything's okay, but that would be horribly rude."

"You could hide down here with me." He wanted her to say yes so badly it had to be unhealthy.

"I can't be impolite, not when they've gone out of their way to be here to help." She raised her gaze to his and speared him with expectation. "You could come up with me. I wouldn't feel so socially inept with you there with me."

Rafe's chest puffed up and lifted him from the chair. Her words made him a giant. They roared every protective cell in his body to life.

He stepped close, the air between them so thick he was surprised it didn't push him backward. Slowly, he lifted his hand and ran the back of his finger down her cheek. The motion, and her widening eyes, incinerated his rabbit-like tendencies of the past few days to ash.

"Let's go be sociable then." His words sounded as rough as sandpaper.

She gulped and nodded. Rafe wouldn't hide away anymore. He'd take Zeke's advice and follow the happiness Piper shined into his life. He'd slay all her fears so she could see the beauty she truly was. He slid his hand in hers and pulled her toward the crowd gathered in the living room.

ELEVEN

PIPER PACED in front of the window in the living room of the ranch house, growling at the blowing snow like a caged tiger. Three whole days and the storm hadn't let up once. Chloe would be in rough shape when they found them. She had barely enough gluten-free food in those stupid Army packets to keep a bird alive.

Piper huffed, stopped her pacing, and set her hands on her hips so she wouldn't wring them. She had to stop thinking about it, had to get her mind off of her cousin's nightmare, but just hanging around the ranch left her little to do and tons of time to think. She'd already done everything she could regarding Chloe's music business and had contacted the hospital to warn them of the situation. She wished Rafe's friends weren't off training or playing in the snow or whatever it was they were doing in the back acres of the property. They had proved great distractions with how they felt a need to tell her embarrassing stories of Rafe and Davis.

She smiled as she thought about the night before and

how it had been filled with laughter. It had amused Piper how her acquaintances in Chloe's band and her new ex-military friends had merged. Who knew artsy-fartsy and American hero could have so much fun together?

She'd finally been able to relax and enjoy the mixed company after she'd convinced Rafe to join them. Her shy nature melted away with his supporting presence. It had been the first night that hadn't been thick with tension since they'd found out Chloe and Jake had crashed. The first night the laughter seemed genuine and not forced.

Piper tipped her head back to gaze at the faint yellow orb of the sun barely showing through the falling snow. She didn't get Rafe. He'd been so concerned after the landslide the night they'd arrived, but hadn't spent more than a minute or two at a time with her since. Then, when she'd asked him to join them, he'd gotten this feral look in his eyes and stuck by her side the rest of the evening.

She'd tried her best to play it cool, to keep her emotions in check and not fall apart at her missing cousin and her confused heart. Tried to keep from shivering every time her skin erupted into goosebumps when Rafe brushed by her. Last night though, when he led her up to the group ... wowzah, talk about tension.

He didn't say or do anything too out of the norm. In fact, it was infuriating how normal he'd been, except for the fact that he'd stayed near her all night. Yet, she'd catch him staring at her and electricity would spike through her body whenever his touch would graze her.

Her mind spun like the carnival rides she loved so much, chaotically switching between hope and doubt.

"Piper, you okay?" Rafe's question turned her from the window.

He emerged from the hall, his appearance back to his normal slick and put together look, instead of the frazzled and tired way he'd appeared last night. She loved how handsome he was with his hair perfectly combed and his beard groomed neatly. She also liked when his hair stood on end from his hands spearing through it. Her new torturous daydream she'd added to the pile from her younger years had her the one messing up his perfect style. She wanted that particular daydream so badly her fingers itched.

She turned back to the window, hoping to hide her fiery face. "Just wondering when this snow will end."

He stepped up beside her, stopping so close the back of his hand rested against hers. His cologne smelled strong and heady. Had he just put it on because he'd see her? She peeked up at him. He didn't give any clue that he had.

"I've been tracking the storm front. It looks like it will clear enough tonight that we can start looking for them tomorrow." Rafe's face didn't reflect the joyful news.

She grabbed his hand and squeezed, her chest tight with his serious face contradicting the vast improvement in the situation. "Tomorrow we find them?"

"Tomorrow, we can start looking." Rafe squeezed her hand and offered her a small smile.

"Why aren't you more excited?"

He ran his free hand over his neck and sighed. "Piper,

I don't want to get your hopes up that we'll find them right off the bat. Locating them in the middle of the mountains after such a heavy snowstorm is going to take time. I've gone over all the data a hundred times, so we have the best triangulation possible for where they went down. It's just ..." Rafe swallowed. "I just don't want to disappoint you if it's not enough, and we don't find them right away."

"You could never disappoint me, Rafe." Dang it. Why'd her voice have to go all breathy and reveal so much?

He gazed at her, his cheek muscle clenching. What did he see when he looked at her? He'd called her beautiful. Did he finally see her as more than Davis's little sister? She bit her bottom lip, and his eyes darted to them.

"Why don't we get out of here for a bit?" he murmured and cleared his throat.

She nodded, her agreement barely audible. "Okay."

He didn't move, though. The air turned thick and sticky between them, like sweet honey encased them, gluing them together. She marveled as his Adam's apple bobbed the distance of his throat. She held her eyes wide as he leaned toward her, not wanting to miss a millisecond.

"What're you guys doing?" Eva, Sam and Zeke's daughter, skipped into the room, followed by Sam.

Rafe jerked away from Piper. He squeezed Piper's hand and walked to the adorable little girl. Piper ran a shaky hand over her hair, her body vibrating from what she assumed was a missed kiss. Sam cringed and mouthed, "Sorry," when Piper collected herself enough to turn away from the window. She smiled and shrugged, waving away the apology.

"My darling fairy princess, I was just convincing the fair maiden to traverse the harrowing paths and venture to the market with me." He bowed dramatically in front of Eva, who giggled into her hands. "Your lowly servant noticed the princess's favorite cheese sticks have depleted, and the fairy queen's ginger ale has run dry. We humbly beg your permission to venture forth on an epic quest to the mart in the land of Wal to procure sustenance."

Piper snorted as Eva flung her arms around Rafe's neck. He was going to be an amazing dad. Jealousy flared in her chest at his future wife, and she lowered her head so she could get her tears under control. Why had she allowed herself to linger over her silly infatuation?

"Permission granted." Eva's serious face pushed a smile up Piper's cheeks, though her heart remained heavy. "Dear knight, can you get the cereal with pink marshmallows, too?" she whispered, but not quietly enough.

"Young lady, he will not, and I've warned you not to ask again." Sam put her hands on her hips.

"Oops." Eva cringed at Rafe, causing him to tip his head back in laughter.

Oh, how Piper loved his laugh.

"I'll see what I can do," Rafe stage-whispered back before tweaking Eva's nose and standing. He cocked his elbow to Piper and winked. "Come, my fair lady, we venture forth."

She rolled her eyes and slid her hand into Rafe's arm.

She forced herself to ignore the warmth that ran from her fingers to her shoulders. Well, tried to ignore.

"Let us know if you need anything else." She smiled at Sam, praying her voice sounded normal.

As Rafe led her down the hall to the garage, Eva's voice followed them. "Uncle Rafe found his princess, didn't he, Mama?"

"We'll see, sweetie." Sam's voice spoke quieter than her daughter's.

"I hope he's not a numskull and messes it up. I like her." Eva's response made Rafe snort.

Piper blushed and scrambled for something to say. "Kids." Seriously, that's all she could come up with?

"Sorry about that." Rafe's neck and ears pinked. "Eva's kind of obsessed."

"She's cute."

Rafe opened his mouth to say something else, then shook his head and snapped his mouth shut. She wanted to ask what he was about to say, but was too embarrassed to push. He opened the truck door for her and shut it with a huff. The drive to the store was quiet. She blamed it on Rafe needing his attention on the slick roads, but knew it was more than that.

When they got to the store, their interaction was limited to small talk about what to get. He made silly jokes with the fruit and teased her when she grabbed the chamomile tea. It wasn't his fun-loving nature growing up, more like a shadow of that.

"I'm going to run to the toy department and grab something for Eva. Sam would kill me if I brought home that cereal, but I can't disappoint Eva either." Rafe's fretting was adorable.

Piper laughed. "You'll spoil her."

"Isn't that what good uncles are supposed to do?" Rafe wiggled his eyebrows up and down. "I plan on being her favorite. Be right back."

Piper shook her head as he darted down the aisle. She stopped in front of the gluten-free section and stared at the selection. She wanted to have all of Chloe's favorites ready for when she made it back.

Piper grabbed items, tossing them into her cart without looking. She squished her lips together at the minimal offerings. Maybe she could talk Rafe into taking her to the natural food store on the other side of town. They'd have a wider selection.

She turned to her cart and froze. A black rose lay across the fruit in the seat of the shopping cart. A chill covered her and her breaths came quickly as she darted her gaze around the vacant aisle. She reached a shaking hand to the note tied with a red ribbon. It crinkled loudly in her ears as she flipped it over.

There's nowhere you can go that I won't find you.

Bile rose up her throat. She worried she'd make a mess in the middle of the aisle.

"Piper?" Rafe's concerned voice broke the hold the rose had on her.

"I think we have a problem." Her words trembled as she pointed her chin to the cart.

Rafe's eyes went wide, then slammed into a glare. "We're leaving."

"But the food."

"We'll get the store to hold it and have someone come get it." Rafe stepped up to the cart, sucking in a breath as he read the note. "I gotta get you safe."

He wrapped his arm around her, and she slumped into him. Her weakness embarrassed her, but she couldn't help it. She was nothing but an awkward woman who stayed behind the scenes. Why in the world would someone be stalking her?

TWELVE

"I CAN'T FIGURE it out, and it's driving me nuts." Rafe spoke into the headset to Zeke as the helicopter flew over Glenwood Springs the next morning toward the mountains to search for Jake and Chloe.

"You will." Zeke had his head leaned against the seat and his eyes closed.

The sun had just started to lighten the dark sky when the helicopter arrived at the ranch. Piper had packed a backpack full of food and medicine for Rafe to take. She'd said she'd be praying for him, and the words had slid into his spirit and buzzed in a low warmth. He knew she meant she'd pray for him to find Chloe and Jake, but he knew she'd worry about him as well.

"The guy must be watching the house." Rafe looked out the window at the sun-kissed tips of jagged land. "I've searched all the feeds, though, and can't figure out where he's holing up."

"The store's security caught nothing?"

"Nada." Rafe huffed and clenched his hands slick

with sweat as he thought about how they'd been so wrong about the stalker. "Just a dude in the same black coat. There aren't any angles of his face, and the snow was too thick to see which vehicle he went to."

"Well, you'll just stick with her until you figure out who it is." Zeke cracked one eye open. "I don't think you'll be complaining too much about that."

A small smile spread across Rafe's face before he stifled it.

"Knew it." Zeke opened his other eye and leaned forward. "You were growling the other night when her friends were over. It was quite amusing. The unflappable Rafe Malone, flapping—and all over a woman."

"Man, you need to get your eyes checked." Rafe adjusted in the seat, uncomfortable with Zeke's observations.

"You just about burned a hole through poor Chet's head with your glares."

"That guy's a menace."

"Why, because he likes Piper?" Zeke smiled knowingly.

"Because he keeps asking her out."

Zeke cocked an eyebrow at him. "Admit it. You're jealous, which means you care—a great deal by the way you practically pounded your chest and grunted 'Mine' the other night."

Rafe snorted and rolled his eyes. "I did not."

"Okay, maybe you didn't, but what about the way you've acted since the stalker left the rose?" Zeke pointed at Rafe. "You're acting all paranoid like the guys can't keep her safe. You're lucky they didn't deck you with all your commands issued before we left."

Rafe rubbed his neck, his ears turning hot. He had acted paranoid. He knew the team would keep her safe. The truth was, he didn't want to leave her safety to anyone else but himself, which was plain dumb considering he'd been the one to leave her alone at the store.

He shivered and looked back out the window. When he had come around that corner and seen her face so pale, he wanted to pull her close and hold her, figuring she got to worrying about Chloe again. Then he'd seen the rose and read the note. He'd almost thrown Piper over his shoulder and run out, driven her so far away and remote no one could find them.

He had been planning to talk to her about what was happening between them. A nice lunch out downtown after shopping while the snow softly fell had been the perfect opportunity to investigate how she felt about him from her own mouth, not just what others were saying. All the hints and words he had thought up had fizzled out of his brain and been taken over by fear.

After getting her home, he decided he couldn't cause even more stress for her. He could wait until all the chaos of Chloe and Jake being lost and the stalker settled to pursue Piper. It'd also give him time to plan his approach, calculate all contingencies, and neutralize all opposition, like the stalker, Piper's brother, and her worries.

"She's the one, Zeke. I don't know how I didn't realize it before, but I can't let anything happen to her."

"Davis will kill you."

Rafe shrugged. "Maybe he'll be happy his best friend and sister are in love."

Zeke snorted. "Not likely."

"Yeah, probably not."

Davis knew all of Rafe's past, after all. Rafe cringed, thinking about some of the things he'd done, the girls he'd dated. The kid he killed. He didn't deserve Piper, that was for sure.

"You deserve her." Zeke's words snapped Rafe's head up.

"I didn't say anything."

"You didn't have to, man. It's written all over you face." Zeke crossed his arms over his chest. "You're one of the best guys I know. If I had a sister, I'd be pushing her at you, begging you to marry her, because I know she'd be treated right."

Rafe shook his head, but a sharp pain speared his heart.

"Two minutes out to first checkpoint," the pilot said over the com.

Rafe cleared out the emotion that clogged his throat. He had a mission that needed his focus, friends to find in the white expanse. Then he'd ramp up his search for the stalker, pulling all his resources, even if they were illegal. When he settled all that, he'd move to the next step in his plan of wooing his best friend's little sister.

Piper glanced around the hospital room later that day, still in a state of shock that not only had Rafe pinpointed

Chloe and Jake's location almost perfectly, but now Chloe's big break might be closer than they ever hoped. Piper couldn't believe she'd held her cool when *Hello, America* had called requesting an interview with Chloe, couldn't believe she'd negotiated time for Chloe and her band to perform. Now, it appeared they'd all be jetting off to New York, and all Piper wanted to do was find a quiet place to escape for a while.

Selfish.

Why did her thoughts always turn that way? This was Chloe's big break, the thing they'd worked so hard and long for. Piper's eyes stung. She couldn't stand herself.

She turned from the room, needing just a moment alone to collect herself.

Derrick stood in the hall, his phone to his ear. His eyebrows rose as he caught sight of her.

"I just need a moment." Piper pointed to the stairwell. "I'll stay right on the other side of the door."

Piper didn't wait for an answer, but stepped quietly to the door to the stairs. Derrick's deep voice and footsteps followed. She huffed. Looked like she wasn't getting space to collect herself after all.

"I'll just stand right here. If you need me, just holler." Derrick pointed to a spot next to the door when Piper turned surprised eyes to him.

Great, now she felt even more uncharitable. She nodded, the hot tears too close for her to say anything. Ducking her head, she scurried out the door. Stalking to the corner of the landing, she leaned her back against it, squeezing her eyes closed to force the tears away.

As one leaked through the barrier, others quickly followed until she silently bawled into her hands. What was her problem? Chloe was safe. Piper should dance with joy, not cry uncontrollably.

"Piper, what's wrong?"

Piper's heart stopped. Why did Rafe have to follow? His soft question had her wiping her hands across her cheeks, praying the stupid tears would just dry up already.

The sound of the door closing and steps toward her made her face heat with embarrassment.

"Nothing. I just got overwhelmed, I guess." She didn't look at him—couldn't, not if she wanted to stop crying.

"Crying your eyes out isn't nothing, Pip." His hand smoothed across her shoulder. "Tell me what's going on."

"I guess I'm just happy. Happy Chloe's safe and her dreams are coming true."

Piper pulled her hands into her sweater and ran the fabric under her eyes. She must look a mess.

"Chloe's dreams are coming true, but what about yours?" Rafe leaned his arm against the wall next to her so he could look at her.

Piper jerked her gaze to his. "I want Chloe to make it. This is what we've wanted for so long."

Rafe shook his head. "I didn't ask what Chloe's dream is. I asked what yours is."

She lifted her hands and shrugged. "This is what I want. I've been doing everything I can for years to help Chloe get to this point."

"Yeah, but what about you, Piper? What have you

done to achieve your dreams?" Rafe's eyebrows lowered over his eyes like she'd upset him.

"I don't know what you are reaching for. This is my dream."

Rafe pushed off the wall and snorted. Piper glared, crossing her arms over her chest. He could huff all he wanted. It didn't change the facts.

"Are you even listening to yourself?" He threw his hands wide. "So you're telling me your lifelong dream has been to make sure your cousin gets hers? That you've never had a dream of your own that wasn't a by-product of someone else's? An afterthought to help someone else get everything they've ever wanted?"

Piper shook her head. He didn't understand. It wasn't like that. It wasn't a bad thing for her to do everything she could to help Chloe succeed.

"Come on, Piper. What is it you've dreamed of for you and only you? There has to be something."

"You want to know my dream?"

"Yes. Yes, I do."

"I never wanted much. Never had any grand plans of stardom." Piper closed her hands into fists as her eyes burned hot again. "All I wanted was to be a wife and mother like my mom was."

Rafe stilled, his eyes widening. Now he knew how silly her thoughts were.

"Stupid, little dream, a joke really when you think of all the men lining up to date me through the years." She scoffed and crossed her arms.

"Seems you have an abundance now." Rafe's joking pinched her heart.

"Yeah, well, it doesn't matter. I buried my dreams long ago." Piper jerked the back of her hand over her wet cheek and pushed past Rafe toward the door.

"Piper—"

"I need to help Chloe get ready to go." Piper yanked the door open and rushed to Chloe's room.

Why'd he have to push? Why couldn't he just leave things be? Piper scrubbed her hand over her face and pasted on a smile as she walked into the hospital room.

At least she hadn't exposed all her dreams, blurting out how they couldn't come true without him. No, she'd thankfully kept her complete pathetic nature to herself ... barely. She had to remember that no matter how many times she caught Rafe staring or how he seemed to find reasons to touch her, his interest was all fabricated in her head. The unfortunate result of a lifelong infatuation she couldn't get under control.

THIRTEEN

"THEY KILLED IT." Piper's breathless words pulled Rafe's attention away from Chloe and her band as they wrapped up their song on *Hello, America*.

Piper's eyes sparkled as she glanced at Rafe, her fingers pressed against her radiant smile. He'd screwed things up with her at the hospital. The last two days had been torture and awkward, their relationship strained.

"All because of you," Rafe whispered, holding her gaze as her eyes widened and her cheeks pinked.

Piper shook her head, turning her attention back to the band.

Why couldn't he have just grabbed her in that stairwell and told her he wanted her to have her dreams with him? He could profess his love for her to Zeke, but then tell her she had lots of options, like it was a bad thing? Eva had called it. He was a numskull.

He'd blown it, and now Piper acted like she always had. He'd propelled himself back into her brother's best friend status. Someone who was fun to have around, but one she didn't share anything meaningful with beyond friendship.

He needed to take a cue from Jake's playbook and do something epic. Jake's declaration of love seemed to put both Chloe and Piper in a dither. Rafe shook his head. Chloe and Jake getting engaged after knowing each other a week seemed insane.

But when one knew, one knew, or at least that's what Rafe was coming to understand. He certainly couldn't believe his eyes had been blind to Piper the last fifteen years. She shouldn't have been able to knock him off kilter, but she did, in a fashion that left his head spinning. Now, all he wanted to do was get this trying trip to New York done and over with so he could take her back to the ranch, figure out who was stalking her, and prove to her he wanted to keep her with him forever.

That last one might be hard considering she barely talked to him anymore.

His shoulders slumped as he followed twenty feet behind her. Their group ventured backstage, and he wanted to give her space to celebrate with her friends.

Derrick came up beside him and slapped him on the shoulder. "Davis's sister sure is special."

Rafe's eyes narrowed at the appreciative tone in Derrick's voice. Great. Someone else bidding for Piper's attention. Rafe couldn't compete with Derrick. Not only was his friend loyal to the core, but Rafe had been told on more than one occasion by women they met that Derrick's deep, smooth voice melted knees like butter left in the sun. Similar sentiments had been said so often that Rafe had just come to accept that if Derrick came out with the guys, all women would preen for his attention.

This time, though, Rafe didn't want to see any preening, especially from Piper.

Derrick held up his hands. "No need to explode my brain with your death glare, man. I know she's yours."

"Sorry." Rafe rubbed his hand over his face. "She's not mine. I screwed things up."

"Yeah, I caught that." Derrick chuckled. "Whatever you did has her dashing out of the chute like an unbroken horse escaping the corral. You just need to lasso that filly and speak soft words until she calms down."

Rafe snorted. Leave it to Derrick to relate this entire situation to cowboying. Though he'd left his rodeo days behind him when he joined the Army, he still exuded western toughness.

"I know she's meant to be yours, but some people haven't gotten the memo." Derrick pointed his chin toward Chet, who approached Piper with a wide smile. "You don't take care of business soon, man, there won't be any business to take care of."

Rafe's eyes narrowed as Chet wrapped his arms around Piper and spun her in a circle. Her face contorted in pain, and she pushed on Chet's shoulder. The man had no consideration for her still bruised back and obvious discomfort. Rafe stomped toward them, his body hot with rage.

Elias, Chloe's drummer, grabbed Chet's shoulder. "Chet, man, step back. You know Piper's still hurt."

Chet pulled Piper closer, his hands running all over her back in exploration. "I'm not going to hurt her."

"Chet, please." Piper's shaking voice blasted all Rafe's thoughts of handling the situation delicately out the window.

"I just want to give you a thank-you kiss." Chet leaned closer, his laugh grating down Rafe's back.

Elias's face tightened, and he pulled again. "Chet, I don't—"

Rafe grabbed Chet by the back of the neck and threw him up against the wall. "Keep your hands off her."

"Back off, jerk, I'm just showing her my appreciation." Chet's face turned crimson.

"Can't you get a clue? She's not interested." Rafe stepped closer, his temper boiling near the surface.

"Her interest in you has obviously passed, so why don't you do your job, you know, watching Chloe. I've got Piper handled." An unkind smile spread across Chet's face as he pitched his voice low so just Rafe could hear. "Nothing like a good heartbreak to make a woman pliable. I should thank you. Whatever you did jump-started my chances with her."

He leaned closer, which Rafe thought was plain dumb. Didn't Chet know Rafe could break him without even trying? Piper tugged on Rafe's hand.

Chet chuckled and pitched his voice low. "Does she taste as good as she smells or do you even know?"

Rafe's arm swung before he even realized what he did. His fist connected with Chet's face, spurting blood onto the floor. Piper stepped between them and pushed on Rafe's chest. He tried to move her out of the way so he could finish pummeling the jerk, but she stood firm.

"Rafe, please, just ... let's go." Her voice cracking

pulled his attention to her crumpled face. "Please, I want to go."

He took a deep breath to tone the rage down, grabbed her hand, and led her toward the exit. He slammed through the door and found the dressing room. The sooner he could gather her stuff and get to the vehicle, the sooner he could take her away to the ranch.

She yanked her hand from his and pushed him. "What was that about?"

He turned around and threw his arms wide. "What do you mean? That guy was being a complete jerk."

"You don't think I could handle it?"

"Are you kidding me? You weren't handling it." Rafe tried to keep his voice down. He really tried.

"Shh, before you make an even bigger scene than you already did." She crossed her arms and glared at him. "He was just excited. This was a big deal, if you haven't clued in yet. Besides, it wasn't so bad having a man want to kiss me. Then you came in with your grunting and bared teeth."

"*Psh*, that's not what I was doing." He rolled his eyes, his blood pressure rising again at her actually wanting the dude's kiss. "Besides, that is not what kissing is supposed to be like, especially since you've told him you aren't interested."

"That's exactly what you were doing." She swatted at the air, ignoring what he'd said. "It was like a pack of feral wolves, and I was the killed prey." Her body went still, and she blinked slowly. "You're jealous."

His mouth turned dry as he looked away. "Am not."

"Yes, yes, you are."

"You shouldn't even be thinking about kissing that jerk."

"Why?" Her eye contact didn't waver, and it unnerved him.

"Why?" Rafe scrambled for an excuse. "What, a stalker isn't a big enough reason to lie low? Or how about that you've already turned him down?"

She stepped closer, too close. Close enough that her heat radiated up his body.

"I don't think that's why you believe I shouldn't be thinking about kissing, well, kissing him." She glanced to his lips, her mouth turning up on one side in a small smile. "I think that little act out there had more to do with you than it did me."

A weight settled in his core, and he rubbed his palm over his heart. "Piper, I just want to protect you."

"Because of my brother?" She bit her bottom lip and looked down, her hesitation spearing his chest.

"No," he whispered and cleared his throat, his heart pounding against his ribs.

She peered back up at him, her eyebrows rising and her gaze questioning.

"Because ..." He swallowed. "I can't stand the thought of you hurt. It's all I think about."

She leaned closer, spreading her hands on his shirt and making his muscles jump like they were pumped with electricity. "You're all I think about too."

She softly touched her mouth to his, her trembling lips contradicting her confident approach. She pulled back, her expression wavering. His well-formulated plan to woo her dissipated like mist in the desert. He grabbed her hips, pulling her back to him, threading his fingers through her belt loops so he didn't hurt her back.

He leaned forward and captured her lips to his. She tasted of mint and hope and a happiness he figured lay well past his reach. He softened his touch when he thought he'd pushed too fast, but she speared her fingers through his hair and held him close. Her touch shot fire through his scalp and to his toes. He curled them to stay standing.

"Piper, I—oh, sorry. I'll just—" Elias stumbled back toward the door, his face and ears bright red.

Piper jumped away from Rafe, her hand touching her mouth. "No, Elias, it's okay." She peeked at Rafe before stepping toward the drummer.

"I ... I just wanted to apologize for not doing more back there." His eyes darted to Rafe before looking down at the ground. "I should've made Chet let go."

"It's okay. He caught us all by surprise." Piper crossed her arms over her chest. "You played great this morning, Elias. I hope this is the break you all have been waiting for."

"If we make it at all, it will be because of you." Elias shrugged. "Thanks for all you've done for the band, Piper. We would still be playing in rundown bars for peanuts if it wasn't for you."

Piper shook her head, and Rafe stepped up and squeezed her shoulder. She deserved to know how others recognized all she'd done to make the band a success. She peeked over at him as he ran circles with his thumb on her sweater.

"She doesn't take flattery very well, man." Rafe

smiled and winked at her. "Has always been more happy in the background instead of the limelight."

"That's what makes her so great." Elias cleared his throat. "Anyway. Thanks, Piper. I'll see you when we start practicing again."

When he'd left the room, Piper brought her hands to her pink cheeks. "How embarrassing."

Rafe shook his head, pulling her back into his arms. "Being caught kissing you isn't embarrassing." He kissed the corner of her mouth that she had tweaked in frustration. "I wouldn't mind being caught kissing you more often."

He brushed a trail of kisses along her jaw to right below her ear. She made a noise in her throat as she leaned her head to the side. Rafe smiled against her skin, glad for once that all his perfect planning went awry. He still needed to get her to the safety of the ranch, but at least now he could stop stressing about hiding his feelings for her.

Chloe's cheerful laugh sounded in the hall, and Piper scrambled out of Rafe's arms. Her face flushed as her gaze darted around the room, freezing when Chloe, Jake, and Derrick walked through the door. Chloe's eyes widened as they bounced from Piper to Rafe.

"What's going on?" Chloe's barely contained smile said she knew exactly what was going on.

"Nothing." Piper's quick response had Rafe cocking his eyebrow at her and looking pointedly at her swollen lips. She rubbed her hand under her ear where he'd just kissed. "We were just getting ready to pack up."

"Right." Chloe rolled her eyes. "Well, let's get going

then. After Rafe bloodied the hallway, the studio is a little eager for us to be on our way."

Piper wrung her hands, her face going pale. "That was all my fault. Should I go talk to them?"

"It wasn't your fault. It was Chet the Jerk's fault, and, no, I took care of it." Chloe stomped to her suitcase and started throwing things in. "Besides, these morning news guys like a little drama, makes their hearts pitter-patter."

It definitely made Rafe's heart do crazy things.

"By the way, when this stalker business is cleared up, we're finding a new guitarist." Chloe shoved a sparkly shirt in her bag with force. "I told Chet to find somewhere else to spread his sleaziness."

Piper's shoulders sagged, and Rafe wasn't fully convinced it was in relief. He wanted to give Piper a break from the craziness of the past week. He wanted to let her have time to not worry about anything, maybe have some double-date movie nights with Jake and Chloe in front of the big screen back at his place he shared with the other guys.

With Chloe insisting the night before that they take a break from the music business until they found the stalker, Piper would have time to just relax. He peeked at her lips. He could think of a few ways to distract her. His smile grew as her neck flushed, and she ducked her head. Yep, he wouldn't mind distracting her at all.

FOURTEEN

PIPER STIFLED her smile as Rafe pulled her closer where they snuggled on the couch. Since leaving New York the day before and arriving at the ranch, he'd been extra attentive, coming up with all kinds of excuses to be with her. The shift in his behavior was startling and over-whelming in the most amazing way. It was like all her daydreams were being rolled out from the scroll she'd tightly wrapped with never-going-to-happen thoughts.

She stared out the second-story floor-to-ceiling window Rafe had pushed the couch up to. He'd said he wanted to stargaze but didn't want her freezing. He'd led her up to a living room upstairs where he'd set up snacks and a thermos full of hot chocolate. He'd even hung a blanket over the entryway, claiming they'd have a better view of the stars if all the inside lights were out. He was right, but she bet there was more to it than that.

Finding privacy in a house full of people proved hard to accomplish. Her cheeks heated, remembering how many times they'd been caught kissing. Being caught by Eva was the worst since she liked to announce it to anyone within shouting distance. Piper smiled as she cuddled closer to Rafe.

The last two hours had been a quiet escape, though, filled with soft conversation and heated kissing. She could get used to this side of Rafe she'd never witnessed before. He rubbed his hand up and down her arm. Her breathing slowed as her eyelids grew heavy. His presence chased all her stress and worry away, leaving her as limp as a contented kitty. Her eyes fluttered closed as she took a deep breath. Hopefully, she wouldn't start purring.

A ding jerked her awake from where she lay stretched next to Rafe on the couch with her head on his shoulder. The sky through the window had gone from black to dark blue streaked with orange and pink, announcing a fast approaching sunrise. How in the world had she fallen asleep and ended practically sprawling on him? Her phone dinged again, and her neck grew hot as she pushed up from her position.

Without opening his eyes, Rafe grabbed her arm and pulled her back down. "Just leave it. It's too early."

Piper pushed back up, scrambling to the far side of the couch where her phone was. Rafe squinted through one eye, his disappointment clear in his tightly pressed lips.

"Since it's early, it's probably important." She swatted his legs as he laid them over hers.

"Just don't take too long. I'm not ready to get up yet."

"You can go back to sleep. I'm going to sneak into my

room." She cringed and shook her head. "I can't have anyone finding us. How—"

Her throat closed as she looked at her phone, choking her words to a halt. A text with an attached folder showed on her locked screen.

UNKNOWN: If I can't have you, no one will.

"Rafe." Her breath stuttered out and her hands trembled so hard she had a hard time getting her phone unlocked.

Rafe was fully awake and by her side in an instant. "What's wrong?" He growled as he read the text, reaching for the phone.

She shook her head, knowing he'd try to protect her from what the attachments were, and unlocked her phone. Taking a deep breath to calm her rapidly frazzling nerves, she clicked on the folder attached to the text. Images that must've been taken through the windows of Zeke's house filled the screen. Pictures of her and Rafe sleeping on the couch, of her changing in her room, and them playing with Eva. She trailed her finger up the screen, scanning them as they kept loading. There had to be dozens of them, all taken since they had gotten back from New York.

Rafe snatched her phone from her and helped her off the couch. "We're leaving, now."

He wrapped his arm across her lower back and led her into her bedroom. Her knees buckled the moment he let her go to shut the curtains, and she slumped onto her bed. Her breaths came in short, quick succession. She needed to slow them down, but she couldn't focus, couldn't think.

Her breaths competed with her heart in a race to her possible demise. She closed her eyes, squeezing them shut, clasping her hands between her knees. She didn't want to die—not when all her dreams looked to come true.

"Honey, I need you to calm down." Rafe's hand smoothed back her hair. "We need to pack, and we can't do that if you pass out."

"I ... can't ... breathe." She pulled at her sweater that wrapped tight around her like a straitjacket. Black spots danced before her face.

"Crap." Rafe sat next to her on the bed and shoved her head between her knees. He rubbed slow, feather-soft circles on her back. "Honey, I need you to breathe like me. Deep breath in ... one ... two ... three and out ... one ... two ... three. Great. Again."

It didn't feel great. It felt as if her lungs were being ripped from her chest. But after a few minutes of his soft touch and guided breathing, her organs decided they'd cooperate.

"Better?" Rafe brushed a tear she hadn't even known she'd leaked from her cheek.

She must look a mess. He kissed her softly on the lips and leaned his forehead against hers. He anchored her, unlike minutes before when she thought she'd fall. She clung to his arms, never wanting to let go.

"It's going to be okay, Piper. I won't let this guy hurt you."

Terror hadn't released its grip on her throat, so she kissed him, leaned back, and gave a firm nod.

"Let's get you packed, then we'll head out." Rafe

stood and pulled her up with him. When she wobbled, he held her tight. "You okay?"

"Yes. I think so."

Rafe pushed her hair behind her ear. "All right. You go grab the stuff you need from the bathroom. I'll get your clothes packed up."

She took a step toward the bathroom, only to do an about-face as he headed toward her dresser. "Rafe, wait." She rushed to his side and pushed the drawer closed. "I'll get this. Could you bring the suitcase in?"

His head tilted to the side as he looked from her to the drawer and back again. A slow smile built and his eyes lit with understanding. Her neck warmed as he chuckled and turned toward the closet.

She yanked open the drawer below, pulled out her long nightgown, then jerked open the drawer Rafe had about opened. Tossing all the new lacy underwear and bras into the nightgown, she tied them up as Rafe sauntered back into the room.

"Is it safe?" Laughter tinged his question.

Piper loved that he found her embarrassment amusing. At least the underwear had distracted her mind from her fear.

"Yes, ornery."

Rafe carried her suitcase with his phone smashed between his shoulder and ear. "I'm taking her to your island. A tropical oasis is just what she needs." He winked at her.

She rolled her eyes and went to the bathroom. She listened to Rafe's conversation as she threw her toiletries into a bag.

"No, I don't want Chloe anywhere near this, and if Jake comes, she'll throw a fit and come as well."

Chloe would throw a fit anyway and demand to join them. Piper couldn't see her cousin letting her and Rafe go off on their own.

"She'll be a handful when she wakes and realizes we're gone, but it's for the best. Hopefully Jake can calm her down." Rafe shoved an armful of clothes into the suitcase as Piper emerged from the bathroom. "Wake Derrick up and tell him he's flying us to paradise."

Rafe hung up the phone and tossed it onto the bed. He pushed his hand through his hair and turned to the closet.

"We'll have to get you some clothes when we get there. All you have is too warm."

"Okay. What's the plan?" Piper tossed her toiletries into the suitcase and moved to the dresser to grab whatever was left in there.

"Zeke has an island that can't be traced to him or the company." Rafe smooshed down her clothes, so she rushed over and pushed him out of the way. "We fly out as soon as we can get packed."

"His plane just crashed." Piper tried to straighten out her clothes, then gave up and zipped the mess in.

"He bought another." Rafe reached for the suitcase.

"Must be nice." Piper wrapped her arms around her stomach. "Chloe's going to flip a brick when she finds out you stole me away."

"Hmm." He wrapped his free arm around her, his voice low and sultry as he whispered against her lips. "Stealing you away. I like the sound of that."

He kissed her. It was quick and hard, but his desperation buzzed against her lips and down her spine. Her mind spun, not used to being the one needing help, so she clung to him, willing to let him take control for a while. Pathetic, really, but she relished the fact that her knight in shining armor actually wanted to rescue her.

FIFTEEN

THE SLAPPING of feet yanked Rafe's attention through the jungle leaves. With careful movements, he pushed the branch down just as a dirt-streaked boy rushed past. Rafe closed his eyes, his heart racing at the added stress the boy no older than ten or eleven carrying a semi-automated weapon presented to the mission. He motioned to those behind him about the added enemy combatant, his stomach souring.

He edged to the side of the building, the rowdy Spanish keeping any noise he'd make covered, not that he'd make any. He paused at the corner, wishing someone else had taken the lead, but grateful he could spare his friends what had to be done. He swallowed, pulling his knife out of its scabbard as they waited for the signal to breach the building.

"Go." The almost inaudible command steeled Rafe's nerves.

He turned the corner on silent feet. The eyes of the boy grew wide as he fumbled for his weapon. Rafe reached for him, hating the men who'd given the kid a gun. Hating himself for what he had to do.

Rafe jerked awake, his computer flying off the little table to land with a soft thump in the seat across from him. His hands shook as he lifted them in front of him, half expecting to see them covered in blood again. He sighed, scrubbing his hands over his face to clear his head and settle his turning stomach.

He glanced around the cabin of Zeke's new jet, his gaze resting on Piper. She'd fallen asleep on the couch, her face relaxed and innocent-looking. What was he thinking? He was too tarnished for someone as pure as her, but he was also too selfish to let her go now that she had opened his eyes. She'd probably kick him to the curb, her crush on him thoroughly destroyed if she ever found out about that last mission.

He got up and pulled the blanket higher that had slipped off her shoulder. He needed a distraction. He went to the galley and snagged a soda, popping the tab as he peeked into the cockpit.

He let the sugary drink slide the roughness from his throat. "Hey, how are you doing up here, Captain Goose?"

Derrick shook his head. "Man, when are you going to let that name go?"

"Not likely, since you still mother us."

"Whatever. Just because I tell you to pick your junk up and get frustrated when the house is trashed, doesn't mean I mother you."

"You're right. It's more how you always ask if we got all

our gear and take us to task when we don't that keeps the Mother Goose name going." Rafe lifted his soda toward Derrick, who sputtered. "You need a drink or something?"

"Yeah, I'd like your smug face on a platter." Derrick turned and raised his eyebrow. "Think you can serve that up for me?"

"Alrighty. A platter of cheese coming right up."

Derrick's deep laugh followed Rafe into the galley. That's just what he had needed, to get someone laughing. He didn't want to deal with the heaviness the dream had settled on him, didn't want to admit that he worried he wouldn't be able to find the stalker. He stacked a soda and some snacks on a tray and went back to the cockpit, placing the tray on the dash and sliding into the co-pilot's seat with a sigh.

"Something on your mind, man?" Derrick checked all the gauges before turning his attention to Rafe.

"Nah." He pulled a drink from the can.

Derrick cocked his eyebrow. "Lighten your load, man. It's a long flight, and I can tell something's bothering you." He reached for a bottle of water and twisted it open. "Dr. D is in the house."

"Dr D?" Rafe snorted.

"It's better than Mother Goose," Derrick said. "I think it'll stick."

Rafe chuckled, but the weight still hung heavy on his shoulders. He peeked back into the cabin to make sure Piper still slept, then grabbed a pack of cookies from the tray.

"What if I don't find this guy?" He twisted the bag in

his hands. "I spent all morning going over everything again, and I keep coming up empty."

"You'll find him. You just need more time." Derrick grabbed an apple. "You're a genius with this stuff."

"What if he's geniuser than me?"

"With English like that, I might agree." Derrick pointed the apple at Rafe. "He's not, few people are, and he won't elude you for long. Plus, us going to the island gives you time. We've gone to long lengths to make it untraceable."

"I hope you're right."

Derrick crunched into his apple, chewed, then peered at Rafe. "So, why don't you tell me what's really bothering you?"

"Why do you think there's something more?" Rafe tossed the bag of cookies back onto the tray.

"Dude, I've spent almost the entirety of a decade with you." Derrick's voice grew solemn. "You haven't been the same since that mission. Seems everything has compounded since Piper arrived."

Rafe grunted and pushed his hand through his hair. "I don't know, D. It's just ... I'm tarnished. The blood of that kid still stains my hands. I figured I'd just hang low, be the best uncle all you guys' kids could have and not have to taint anyone else with what I'd done. Then Piper ..."

Emotion strangled Rafe's words in his throat. Shoot. He swallowed and turned his attention out the side window, blinking to clear the sting from his eyes.

"Then Piper came, and you realized being uncle wouldn't be good enough." Derrick's voice pitched low.

Rafe sniffed and pushed his words out of his aching throat. "She's just too naïve, too wholesome. She's hardly even dated, and here I am a royal flirt and a kid killer."

"You are not a kid killer. The men who forced that boy into their army were."

"I could've used non-lethal force."

"Not without compromising the mission. If you hadn't done what needed to be done, that kid could've come around, alerted that entire complex of our presence, or thrown that grenade he had strapped to his pants and killed us all. It was war. We all did things we wish we hadn't had to. Don't make you tarnished, man. You still grappling with it proves your humanity—that you were fighting on the side of good."

"If I'm so good, then why does it haunt me still?"

"You remember how Hunter used to tell us those tales of King David and Joshua and his men from the Bible?" Derrick continued when Rafe nodded. "He told us because he wanted us to remember that those men of God had to do violent things. There's a reason David wrote a bulk of the Psalms. Even when he did everything right, he was still haunted, as you say."

"Man, I'm nothing like David. He was a man after God's own heart."

"You're right. You aren't an adulterer, murderer, or womanizer."

Rafe's head flinched back, and his thoughts froze.

"You remember that prayer Hunter prayed over us on so many missions, the soldier's prayer from Psalm 91?" Derrick placed his hand on Rafe's shoulder.

Rafe could hear Hunter's voice in his head, his strong

words full of determination and belief. It was Hunter's unassuming walk with God that had made Rafe look at his own faith with regret. It was Hunter's example that had slowed Rafe's participation in the dating scene. He hadn't called dating off completely like Hunter had, but Rafe hadn't taken it as lightly either. But mostly it was that prayer that Hunter would pray that seeped into Rafe's soul and grabbed on tight.

"Let Your truth be my shield and buckler against the fiery darts—the lies—of the enemy." Derrick's rich voice eased into Rafe's gut, calming the pain that had settled there. "Stop choosing the enemy's lies, man, and let God's truth shield you." He squeezed his shoulder. "I need to stretch my legs. Holler if anything starts beeping."

Rafe bobbed his head once, then stared out the window. He asked God to show him the truth. Immediately, Rafe's heart filled with a warmth that spread through his body, like a hug from strong arms. Gooseflesh erupted across his skin, and he shivered with the sudden sense of God's love. Rafe bowed his head, thanking God for His mercy.

He sniffed and dashed his finger under his eye. Lifting his gaze out the window, he felt lighter than he had in over a year. He also realized that he had to tell Piper. He prayed she'd understand. He didn't think she'd hate him because of what had happened, but he'd also witnessed people's reactions to the atrocity of war. Often he was left surprised.

Piper stared at herself in the mirror, turning this way and that as she inspected her bathing suit. The dark blue halter top one-piece Chloe had forced Piper to buy in Steamboat made her feel like she'd stepped out of the fifties. She loved the way it fit with its full coverage of the girls up top and the adjustable side ties on the bottom that let her keep her back side from hanging out. Now, she questioned if instead of trendy, she just looked old-fashioned. Why couldn't Zeke's private getaway be some-where colder, like Greenland or Antarctica?

They'd arrived at the island after a thirteen-hour flight interrupted by quick stops to refuel. When it appeared like they were landing on the ocean, she had gripped the armrest so hard, she worried she left finger-nail marks in the leather. Turned out, Zeke's island not only had a house worthy of every luxury TV show out there with its sleek architecture, perfectly decorated rooms with stellar views of the ocean, and infinity pool, but it also came with a landing strip.

Derrick had crashed in his bedroom the instant they had walked through the door, while Rafe told her to change into her swimsuit, claiming the two of them needed to burn off some energy swimming. He may have extra energy to burn. He always had. She, on the other hand, just wanted to lock the door, climb into the soft white bed, watch the waves as they slapped lazily against the sandy beach, and pray this nightmare would end.

She pushed her fingertips against her eyes. Hiding under the covers wouldn't change anything. It'd simply make Rafe even more concerned about her. She didn't want to add more for him to worry about, so she'd pull on her big girl panties and act like her mind wasn't unraveling.

She yanked her hands through her hair, pulled it into a messy bun on the top of her head, and wrapped a towel around her waist. She took her time making her way to the porch and admired how the inside of the house blended seamlessly with the view. She'd have to ask Rafe if a caretaker lived here, because the place was immaculate.

As she made her way to the beach down a series of steps and decks set up with inviting couches filled with colorful pillows, she told herself she didn't need to be nervous. She'd swam in the pond with Rafe almost every day of the summer growing up. Her stomach felt empty and nauseous at the same time, and the intense desire to flee back up the steps and fashion a muumuu out of the comforter filled her.

Stepping onto the beach, she curled her toes into the warm sand. A salty breeze teased her hair and cooled her sweaty skin. Okay, maybe it wouldn't be so bad.

Rafe hollered and waved from far out in the ocean. She held her hand over her eyes, wishing she had thought to bring a hat. She snorted. Who was she kidding? No thought had gone into her frantic packing. She half wished she would've missed snagging her swimwear as she'd shoved things into her suitcase.

As Rafe swam back to shore in his powerful and smooth-stroked way, Piper ventured to the palm-frond roofed cabana. A hammock swung slightly where it stretched between two of the dark wooden posts. More couches surrounded a table, and she imagined herself lounging in them for hours reading. On the table sat a tray of tropical fruit and other snacks. A cooler was tucked under the table. She smiled, touching her neck at how thoughtful Rafe had been while she fretted in her room.

Splashing drew her gaze to him as he stepped out of the water. The sun sparkled on his wet skin, and Piper averted her gaze. Wowzah. He hadn't looked like that in high school. Her hands slicked with sweat, and she twisted them in the towel to dry them.

"Hey, Pipster. Ready to take a dip?" Rafe jogged up to the cabana and shook his head, sending water flying all over her.

She shrieked and held up her hands, laughing. Rafe had done that as a teenager. It comforted her to know that not everything about Rafe had changed.

"I won't need to go swimming now that you've soaked me." Piper flicked water off her arm.

"I could soak you more." He snaked his arm around her back and pulled her close. "Did you put sunscreen on, my fair-skinned siren?"

She couldn't find her voice as he ran the back of his fingers down her neck and over her shoulders. She shook her head.

"Well, let's get your delicate skin protected. I don't want you red as a lobster like that one time you and Chloe sunbathed all afternoon." Rafe stepped back and grabbed the sunscreen spray on the table.

Piper laughed. She'd forgotten about that disaster. She held out her hand. "Spray some here so I can get my face."

Rafe complied, then motioned with his finger for her to turn around. He smoothed his hand over her shoulders. His touch heated her skin hotter than the tropic sun.

"Your bruises seem to be healing well."

Piper smeared the sunscreen over her face and ears. "It doesn't hurt much anymore, just if I bump up against something wrong."

"That's good." He tossed the can on the couch. "I'm just going to get a drink, then we can go splash with the fish."

"What kind of fish are there?" Piper unwrapped her towel, looking out at the water in anticipation.

She hoped there were bright fish they could watch, but also didn't like the thought of certain slimy creatures swimming between her feet. Chloe had forced her to watch too many scary movies that involved the open water for Piper's liking. Her imagination had more than enough situations without the help of those movies.

When Rafe didn't answer, she turned her head his direction. He'd frozen as he'd lifted the bottle of water to his lips, his eyes wide as he looked her up and down. She curled her fingers into her palm so she wouldn't fidget.

"Um, uh." He blinked rapidly and shook his head.

He jerked his gaze from her and chugged from the bottle. She stifled a smile and turned back to the water. Maybe she'd changed a lot since high school, too.

He cleared his throat and thunked the water on the table. "There're lots of tropical fish, plus sting rays, jellyfish, maybe turtles. We can go fishing later, try to get us some dinner."

"Sharks?" She raised her eyebrow.

He tipped his head back and laughed. "Maybe, but I'll protect you." He grabbed her hand and pulled her toward the water. "Come on. Stop stalling."

The warmth of the water surprised her as she waded into the ocean. The clear water allowed her to see the entire ocean floor where small fish darted this way and that. The tension of the frantic day rippled away as the waves lapped against her thighs. Zeke having a tropical island might be the best way to escape ever.

Rafe wrapped his arms around her, a silly grin on his lips. "Ready?"

"Huh?" Her brows furrowed, then winged up as Rafe fell backward with her in his arms. "No!"

She came up sputtering. Rafe's laughter filled the area. Not the sound she'd heard over the past week that had lost its authenticity, but the sound that had embedded into her very being as a young teen. It was the sound of home, the sound she had craved the years he'd been away in the military. She had wondered if he'd lost it in the trenches of protecting freedom. He could dunk her a hundred times if it pulled that particular laugh from the depths of wherever he'd buried it.

SIXTEEN

THE FAINT SPUTTER of a boat motor approaching pulled Rafe's attention from the computer screen. Derrick had left earlier to pick up someone on the mainland, but he hadn't been gone long enough to get there and back. Rafe pushed back from the table, rolling his neck that was tight from too many hours staring at the screen, and checked his sidearm.

After two days of untangling leads, he still had little to show for it. This guy was good, and it scared Rafe more than he'd ever been before. No one was perfect, though, so Rafe would keep following rabbit trails for years until he found the crack that let him bust the mystery wide open.

"That must be Derrick." Piper tossed the book she was reading onto the couch and moved to the windows. "I'm betting its Chloe Zeke said to go pick up. She probably nagged them so much they relented."

"Could be. The message didn't say." Rafe tried not to stare at Piper but failed.

She'd been gorgeous back in Colorado with her long sweaters and leggings. Piper in breezy sundresses and shorts and tank tops looked like some kind of Greek goddess from ancient myths come down to grace humanity with her presence. He'd had to ask Jesus for the strength to be honorable several times in the last few days. It hadn't kept him from researching getting hitched in the area. That it was relatively easy hadn't helped his mind from wondering what-if.

Rafe joined her at the window. "Not Derrick. The motor isn't right."

Piper looked at him as if he'd grown three heads. "The motor isn't right?"

He laid his arm across her shoulder, needing to pull her closer. "Dear Piper, as a man, an impressive specimen of man I might add, I have the unique ability to distinguish whether motors are the sophisticated purr of a luxury speedboat like Zeke's or the high-whine of a more simple motor of the delivery man."

She rolled her eyes, but leaned into him. "Please."

Rafe pointed to the end of the island just as Emori Bola, the island's caretaker, trolled around the corner in his small fishing boat that should have gone to Davey Jones's locker years ago. Its sputtering engine always signaled his arrival. Though Zeke paid the man well for taking care of the place, he still insisted on living like he always had. Rafe liked Emori—liked his easy laugh and silly jokes.

"Come on." Rafe guided her toward the door. "I want you to meet someone."

He loved how right she felt tucked close to his side,

her arm wrapped around his waist. He loved how he could just turn his head and kiss her. He gave into temptation and pressed his lips into her hair, lingering a moment to breathe in the salty smell of the ocean remaining from their earlier swim and her perfume that still drove him nuts. He loved her ... period. He needed to tell her, but first he had to stop being a chicken and tell her about what he'd done on that last mission. She deserved to know the truth about him before anything went further.

They reached the dock just as Emori slowed the motor down. The man's smile stretched wide across his face as he waved.

Emori grabbed a dock line and tossed it to Rafe. "My friend, why did the fish blush?"

Rafe caught the line and tied a cleat hitch knot to secure the boat to the dock as Emori cut the engine. "I don't know. Why?"

"Because it saw the ocean's bottom." Emori rocked back, a full belly laugh filling the air.

"I'll have to remember that one for my niece." Rafe's chuckle dried up as a boy stood from behind Emori.

Though the kid's hair curled tight against his head instead of hanging long and dirty around his face, he looked identical to the boy that haunted Rafe's dreams. He stumbled backward, his hands shaking at his sides. He had the frightening urge that he'd throw up right there on the dock.

Emori glanced from Rafe to the boy, his brows furrowing low over his eyes. "Rafe, I'd like to introduce you to my son, Timi. We finally convinced his mama he was old enough to help me."

"Hey." Rafe's mouth was dry like he'd swallowed a pound of sand. "Nice to meet you."

His voice sounded rough and hollow in his ears. *Pull it together.* He jerked when Piper threaded her fingers through his. She gazed up at him with her bottom lip worried between her teeth.

He motioned toward the crates in the boat. "You need help unloading those?"

"Nah. That's what Timi is here for." Emory waved Rafe off.

Rafe stepped backward, hardly containing the desire to run far and fast from the boy. Piper followed, her hand tight in his. He needed to get away to the other side of the island. No, the other side of the world.

"Rafe, what's wrong?" Piper's voice trembled.

He hated that he'd caused her even more worry. She'd been relaxing, the tension leaving her more with each day that passed. Now he'd gone and piled it all back on her weary shoulders.

"Let's go for a walk." He avoided answering her, and Piper, being the kindhearted person she was, didn't push.

He took off for the hill, barely keeping his pace contained to a walk. She kept up with him, occasionally patting his hand like she felt she needed to let him know it was all right. It wasn't, of course, but he dreaded telling her why.

They reached the top of the hill, and he let go of her hand. He didn't want to be touching her when he told her. He knew he'd be tempted to squeeze her hand if she decided to pull away. He didn't want her to feel pressured to stay—pressured to love him when whatever image she had of him dissipated like mist in the morning sun.

"Wow, is that a cannon?" Piper crossed to the stacked line of rocks that used to be a fort from the time of pirates and British rule.

"Yeah." Rafe snatched at the opportunity to delay the inevitable a few seconds longer. "Zeke has been researching the history of this island, trying to find out what used to be here. The most he's been able to find so far is that it used to be claimed by some pirate named Frankie "The Shadow" Asheton. It's become an obsession."

He paced around the structure and leaned against the crumbling wall while she bent and examined the rusted cannon. The ocean stretched out into the horizon as far as he could see, and the birds' songs floated up from the coconut trees below. He closed his eyes and ran his hands across the rough surface of the rocks, letting the peace of the landscape ease the tension from his muscles.

The sound of Emori's boat motor jerked Rafe's eyes open as the vessel skipped across the water's blue surface. Timi leaned against the bow, his arms spread wide and his smiling face tipped to the sky. Rafe's heartbeat increased as he stared at the boy, willing himself to see the differences so he'd stop freaking out.

"Are you ready to tell me what's going on?" Piper leaned against the wall next to him.

Though he didn't look at her, her stare pulled the words up his throat before he'd prepared himself to speak. "Timi reminds me of someone. A boy ... a boy I killed in South America."

"Oh, Rafe." She placed her hand on his, but he pulled it away, shoving it shakily through his hair.

"It was on a mission, rescuing a family that had been kidnapped. We were about to breach the building where the family was held when a boy, probably around ten years old or so, ran up dressed in fatigues and carrying a semi-automatic rifle." He chanced a peek at Piper's reaction.

A pained expression crossed her face. "What happened?"

"In order to breach the building, we had to neutralize the guards." Rafe shrugged like it hadn't left a hole in his soul. "I was lead, so ..."

He couldn't voice the rest.

"That must've been hard." She stepped closer, her hand sliding up his arm. "It explains a lot."

"About what?" He swallowed, not sure if he wanted to know.

"Where your laughter went." She placed her palm on his cheek, and he leaned against it.

Rafe's eyes stung, and he shook his head. "I laugh."

"Yeah." She smiled sadly. "But not like you used to. Not where your joy and love of life infects those around you. Now, it's like you laugh and joke so others won't see what's missing."

Well, shoot. Rafe closed his eyes, horrified as a tear raced down his cheek. How had she noticed? He sniffed, but the action didn't stop the next drop from joining its traitorous friend in his beard.

She leaned over and kissed his cheek. "I'm discovering the depths of you, Rafe Marcus Malone. You can't hide from me. And you know what?" She paused, and he shook his head, not able to speak around the boulders lodged in his dry throat. "I love you more now than I ever have, and that was a lot, I can assure you."

He opened his mouth, but words wouldn't emerge. He wanted to tell her he loved her, tell her he felt whole when she was around, but his throat was too tight to get the words out. So, he wrapped his arms around her, pulled her as close as he could, and buried his face against her neck. He'd finally found home here by her side. His mission now was to stay here the rest of his life.

Piper clung to Rafe's hand as they made their way back to the house. She'd well and truly done it. She'd thrown her heart right out into the open, exposing the depth of herself to him.

She peeked over at him. He hadn't said he loved her back. He didn't have to, not really. She saw his love in the soft expression in his eyes. She felt it in the desperate way he clutched her close.

Strange thing, this sense that she held him up. When had she become the lifejacket that floated him to the surface—buoyed him back to himself? She shook her head at the absurd thought, but the image stuck. It both elated and frightened her. He was the hero, not her. She'd never been anything but the awkward sidekick.

With Rafe, though, she wondered if she could save

him. She could never truly heal the scars his service to the country had left. Only Jesus could do that. Yet, she got the impression as he told her what he'd had to do that he held his breath for her reaction. Maybe her loving him no matter what memories haunted him would help him recover the part of his heart that had shattered?

She could do that. Pray that God would heal Rafe's hurts while loving him through his restoration. Purpose fluttered like a hummingbird on steroids in her chest.

The house came into view, so she pulled him to a stop. He glanced around, then peered at her, his eyebrow cocking up in question. She stepped closer, pressing her hand over his heart. The heat of his skin leeched through his thin cotton shirt and warmed her palm. She closed the distance between them, wrapping her other arm around his back, and pressed one soft kiss to his lips.

His whisper was soft against her mouth. "You're amazing."

Her smile bloomed wide as she kissed him again. He groaned, wrapping his arms around her, but he touched her lips like they were delicate glass. His gentleness filled her heart with warmth at the same time his steely embrace tingled her toes with excitement.

"Piper?" Davis's voice jolted her from Rafe.

"Crap," Rafe muttered, his hands flexing on her hips before letting loose.

She turned, her ears turning hot as her brother's glare bounced between her and Rafe. "Davis? What are you doing here?"

No, no, no! Her brother couldn't be here. She instantly felt guilty. It'd been over a year since she saw him last, but he would ruin everything between her and Rafe. She darted her eyes to Rafe to gauge his reaction. Sweat dotted his forehead that hadn't been there a moment ago.

"I have leave time saved up and came to help." Davis crossed his arms. "Looks like I got here just in time."

She fiddled with her collar as her face went from warm to hot. She couldn't decide if she was embarrassed or mad. *Think, Piper, think.*

"It's so good to see you." She pasted on a smile and rushed to him for a hug.

It wasn't a lie, not really. She had missed him terribly the last few months. Yet, Davis's stiff posture and the scowl he flashed to Rafe before opening his arms to embrace her screamed trouble. If he made a big deal about this, she might have to push aside her docile little sister role and beat some sense into him.

"Glad you're here, man." Rafe stepped up with his hand outstretched.

Davis tucked her under his arm, then extended his other to grip Rafe's. "Yeah, well, I couldn't just sit and wait for news anymore. When my last mission finished, I put in the request to leave."

"Wish Zeke would've told us you were coming." Piper squeezed his side, hoping to ease his tension. "I thought that Chloe had bugged them to let her come and that was who Derrick had to pick up."

"Hmm." Davis squeezed her shoulder. "I bet you would've liked a warning."

She'd kill him.

She smiled, pinching him and hoping he'd take the hint. "Come on. Let's get you settled."

She pulled him toward the house, peeking back at Rafe, who winked at her. Her agitation eased a little. She bit her lip. Maybe this wouldn't be so bad. They'd all been friends forever. Maybe her brother wouldn't flip a brick.

She squeezed his side and kissed his cheek as the joy of seeing him again finally took hold. "I can't believe you're here." She hugged him again when he gave her a weak smile. "I've missed you so much."

His chuckle loosened the tenseness in her stomach even more. "I've missed you too, Pipstick."

"How long is your leave?"

"Well, since it's my transitional leave, I guess forever." Davis jiggled her shoulder.

"What?" Piper's voice came out a squeak. Was he saying what she thought he said?

"When'd you decide to retire?" Rafe stepped up on her other side, his hands shoved into his pockets.

"Well, you guys seemed to be having a lot of fun in the private sector. Figured it was my turn to give it a go." Davis smiled, but Piper saw a tightness in his eyes that had never been there before.

She pushed the worry away. He was here and wouldn't be going back to the Army. With both Rafe and Davis out of the military, she could relax after ten years of constant worry. Now, if they could just find her stalker, life, for once, might be perfect. She squeezed her brother tighter. She'd make sure his sudden appearance brought joy to this crazy, tropical getaway.

SEVENTEEN

"I'M GOING to go get my swimsuit on so we can go spear fishing." Piper's palm tapped on Rafe's back as she walked past. "I'll be quick."

"Take your time." Rafe forced a smile, building back up all those false walls she'd just torn down up on the hill.

Rafe sat on the stool of the kitchen island, taking a slow pull on his iced tea. His muscles coiled, twitching as he waited for Davis to show his true reaction to finding Rafe snogging Piper. His lip tweaked up. Man, who would've guessed the quiet, sweet Piper could be such an amazing kisser?

"What the heck, man?" Davis turned on Rafe the instant Piper disappeared down the hall and pulled Rafe from his daydreaming. "You're supposed to be looking out for her, not chewing on her face!"

"Listen, Davis, a lot has happened the last few weeks." Rafe set the glass down.

Davis's eyes closed to slits, and his jaw tightened. "Just how much has happened?"

Shoot. Wrong thing to say. "Nothing. Nothing like that. Just kissing, I swear." Rafe stood casually from the stool, not wanting to be stuck sitting if Davis went ballistic. "She's ... Man, she's amazing."

"I bet so. Kind of convenient being stuck on an island with someone who's been completely fascinated with you since middle school." Davis uncrossed his arms and took a step closer. "Easy entertainment, right? Good ol' Rafe, always up for a good time."

"What? No."

"That's low, Malone, even for you."

Rafe's chest heated, and his fist clenched. "What's wrong with you, man? I put the party life behind me years ago, and you know it."

"Have you found her stalker?"

"No, not yet."

"So you're wasting time, sucking face and going fishing while the guy who's been terrorizing her roams free?" Davis got right in Rafe's face, his anger radiating off of him in waves.

Rafe shook his head. What had happened to his best friend? Davis had never been like this before.

"You need to step back, Davis." Rafe relaxed his muscles and spoke softly, trying to dispel the tension filling the room. "I'm doing everything I can, have programs running nonstop untangling this guy's trail. I'm on it, man." He'd just leave out the part of coming up empty for later. "But Piper and I have something special.

You should be happy that two people you care about found each other."

Davis poked Rafe in the chest. "You'll just hurt her. Have fun for a while, then throw her off for the next girl toy."

Rafe's heartbeat grew loud in his ears. "I'd never hurt her. I love her, man. I'm spending the rest of my life loving her."

The punch came hard and fast, exploding pain along his jaw and stars in front of his eyes.

"Hey! Whoa, now." Derrick sprinted into the room, stepping between Davis and Rafe. "I know Rafe's jokes can be bad, but they aren't worth decking him over."

"He better be joking, or he'll get more than a slug to the face." Davis pushed against Derrick's hands.

Rafe shook his head to clear the ringing and stared Davis down. "It's no joke, Davis. If she'll have me, I'm marrying Piper." He stretched his jaw. Dang, that hurt. "You better calm yourself down, man. Piper's had enough stress over the last three weeks to last a lifetime. You better not add more."

Piper's footsteps sounded in the hall. Derrick glanced between Rafe and Davis, his eyebrows rising in question. Davis stepped back and jerked his shirt straight.

"We good?" Derrick patted Davis on the shoulder.

"Yeah." Davis turned toward the kitchen. "For now."

Just great. Rafe's hands trembled. He'd expected Davis to get defensive. He'd always wanted to keep Piper protected in bubble wrap. This intense of a reaction spiked pain not just across Rafe's face but also through his heart. He rubbed his chest as Piper rushed into the room.

"Okay, I'm re—" She stopped short, her eyes bouncing between the three men. When her gaze landed on Davis, her eyes narrowed. "What's going on?"

"Nothing." Rafe smiled widely, then tempered it when she cocked one eyebrow. "Just a little roughhousing to say hello."

Her eyes darted to his cheek and widened. He needed to fix this. He didn't want her to have to worry over him and Davis, not when she'd been so relaxed.

He stepped up to her and put a hand on her back. "Listen, why don't you go fishing with Derrick and Davis. I want to stay behind and analyze the latest reports."

"Okay." Her shoulders dropped before she hitched them back up with a weak smile.

He leaned closer, not wanting to see the disappointment on her face. "Maybe after you get back, we can go for another walk."

She reached out and squeezed his hand. "I'd like that."

Davis thunked his glass down hard on the counter with a huff. She glanced at her brother and growled. Rafe chuckled, squeezing her hand before heading toward the office. Maybe she'd sort out Davis so Rafe wouldn't have to.

"So, Derrick, it looks like we're stuck with the grump." Piper's words forced a snort from Rafe.

"Looks like." Derrick's deep chuckle followed.

"Whatever. Let's go fishing." Davis's grumble was the last thing Rafe heard as he closed the office door.

He crossed the room, slid into the leather chair, and woke up the computer. The boat motor firing up drew Rafe's gaze out the window as Zeke's speedboat eased away from the dock. Derrick said something that made Piper's head fall back and her mouth to gape wide in laughter. Even Davis's face lost its hardness.

Rafe ran his palm over the emptiness that settled in his chest. Davis couldn't mean what he'd said. He knew Rafe had put his partying life away shortly after graduating high school. Sure, he'd go out dancing and hanging out with the guys when off duty, but he definitely wasn't a playboy. Davis didn't know what he was talking about.

Rafe would never hurt Piper. He tore his gaze away from the boat and pulled up the programs he'd had running. He'd just tone things down with her, give Davis some time to adjust. His best friend had to be struggling with something more than just Rafe's relationship with Piper. Davis had to be. Otherwise, Rafe would have to decide between following his heart or saving his oldest friendship. No, he shook his head. He had to fix whatever had Davis's boxers in a bunch, because deciding between the two might just rip Rafe's heart out for good.

"Piper, why did the fisherman suddenly turn his boat?" Derrick asked as he started the boat up.

"I don't know. Why?" Piper prayed he could ease the tension that radiated from her brother.

Rafe hadn't fooled her with the whole "we're wrestling" bit. He and Davis may have played rough growing up, but they'd rarely come to blows. Maybe if Davis would just relax, she could get him to tell her what the heck was going on.

"Just for the halibut." Derrick laughed as he said the punchline.

The joke startled her in its ridiculousness. Her head fell back, and her laugh exploded loudly across the water. Davis snorted next to her. She darted her gaze to him. His face had relaxed, and his lips tipped up on one side. Praise God for Derrick Nicholson.

"What does one tide pool say to another?" Derrick's smile stretched across his face, and Piper couldn't help but do the same.

"What?" Her cheeks hurt, waiting for the answer.

"Show me your mussels." Derrick wiggled his eyebrows up and down.

She shook her head as she clutched her sides. The jokes were horrible, but also exactly what she needed to calm down.

"Wait, I've got another." Derrick paused for effect. "What do sea monsters eat?"

Piper wiped a tear from her cheek. "I'm afraid to ask."

"Fish and ships."

Davis leaned back against the seat, his arm bouncing against hers in silent laughter. "Man, those stink."

"I know, right?" Derrick maneuvered the boat to the coral reef.

"Did Emori tell you those?" Piper asked.

"Yeah. That man is full of good ones."

"Full of something." Davis snorted.

Piper turned her face to the salty wind as it whipped

through her hair. She let it slush off the heated energy that still clung to her. Her brother was here and done with the Army. So what if he was cranky? He'd get over it, eventually.

Her fingers chilled as she peeked at her brother. Had something happened to Davis? Was that why he wasn't acting like himself? She chewed on the inside of her cheek. What if she couldn't help him see reason? Her relationship with Rafe couldn't possibly bother Davis that much. Could it?

"Pip, what are you thinking?" Davis scowled up at the house. "Rafe's just going to hurt you."

"You're wrong, Davis." Piper shook her head.

"No, I'm not. You don't know him like I do."

"I know him."

"You think you do, but he's not the guy you put on a pedestal all those years ago." Davis leaned forward, placing his arms on his legs and clenching his hands together. "He's a player, Pip. He's got a line of women with their hearts broken because of him."

"Maybe he used to be a player, but he's not anymore."

"Why? Because he told you?" Davis snorted.

"Why are you acting like this?" Piper crossed her arms over her chest, her insides heating in anger. "He's your best friend."

"Some best friend, taking advantage of my little sister."

Piper poked Davis in the arm. "He didn't take advantage of anyone. In fact, he tried to keep his distance because he knew you'd be upset." Piper took a deep breath so she would keep from shouting. "I'm not the naïve little girl anymore, Davis. I love him, and he loves me, too. Please, can't you be happy for us?"

"Not gonna happen." Davis pushed off of the seat and moved to the front of the boat.

She peered back toward the shore and blinked the tears from her eyes. She didn't want to cause her brother to fight his best friend. Davis should be ecstatic that she and Rafe were together. If they got married, Davis could call Rafe a brother for real.

If Davis never got over it, then what? Could she live with herself if her brother disapproved? Since their parents' deaths, she had looked to him for approval. She'd tried so hard to earn his smile and "good job," not that he had required it from her. She put a hand over her stomach. Just the thought of disappointing Davis rolled her gut.

Yet, she couldn't lose Rafe either. She looked up toward the sky to ease the sting in her eyes. No, not when she'd seen how her love was healing him. There was no way she could go back to being just the tag-along little sister now.

"Come on, Piper. What is it you've dreamed of for you and only you? There has to be something."

Rafe's words echoed in her brain. Her gaze swung toward the crumbling fort on the hill. Rafe was her dream. A life full of love and family had been her hope. She wanted to have Rafe's gaze warm her to her toes for the rest of her days. She wanted to keep close the way she felt cherished when he was around. She longed for babies to snuggle and grandchildren to adore. She wanted that all with Rafe. Her heart wouldn't have it any other way.

The only obstacle to her dream was Davis. She set her jaw and darted her gaze to her brother. She couldn't be her passive self this time, not when so much hung in the balance. She refused to allow his anger to crumble what she and Rafe had like the remains on the hill. She also refused to let her brother lose the best friend he'd ever had.

She pushed her shoulders back and lifted her chin. If she could coordinate Chloe's career to rocket her to stardom, she could figure out how to get her knucklehead brother to see her and Rafe as a good thing.

EIGHTEEN

RAFE SAT IN THE HAMMOCK, swinging while he stared at the ocean. All the joy and hope that had built within his heart had shriveled and dried since Davis had arrived two days earlier. Davis's well placed barbs against Rafe's character had dug deep into his skin. The reminders of his past brought up memories of events even Davis didn't know about and covered Rafe's throat with guilt every time he found himself with Piper.

He sighed and pushed against the decking of the cabana, sending the hammock to swing higher. Davis was right. Rafe didn't deserve Piper. For the life of him, though, he didn't want to let her go. Was he being selfish in wanting to hold tight to her? Would he end up hurting her like Davis said?

"Penny for your thoughts?" Piper's sweet voice slid down his spine, releasing all the tightness bound there.

Her words registered, and his back bunched right back up. He couldn't tell her his worries.

Not yet, at least.

Maybe never.

He cleared his throat. "I was just thinking how calm it was here. Makes one almost forget there's a world still grinding just across those waters."

"Can I join you?" She twisted her hands in the bright sarong she'd wrapped around her waist.

Her nervousness clenched his gut. He was a jerk. She had to know that his mind was at war. He'd hoped to hold his thoughts close, but he couldn't seem to hide anything from her. That fact both unnerved and calmed him at the same time.

He nodded and stopped the hammock, scooting to the side so she could sit next to him. He didn't dare open his mouth or he might spew all his doubts right onto her lap. He desperately wanted to ease her burden, not add to it. So far, he'd done a lousy job at accomplishing that end.

"I'm worried about Davis." Her words caused Rafe's breath to whoosh out.

She hadn't been worried about him? Maybe he was doing a better job at hiding than he thought. He draped his arm across her shoulder as she sat next to him. She snuggled close and sighed.

"Yeah, me too." Rafe ran his fingers up and down her arm. The smoothness of her skin beneath his rough fingers soothed him.

"He's so cynical." She pulled her legs up to her body like she needed to protect herself. "He's never been like this before."

Hurt laced through her worried tone. Rafe's neck heated, and he barely held back the urge to rush up to the house and beat Davis. Why'd he even come if all he was going to do was make everyone miserable?

"Us grunts all have different ways we deal with what we've witnessed. Some manage better than others. Some guys lash out in anger, some become reclusive, pulling away from everyone to protect themselves." Rafe thought of Jake and how Chloe had yanked him from his dark solitude.

"Others hide in plain sight, pretending everything's all right." Piper spread her hand across Rafe's chest and curled her body in a hug around his side.

He grabbed her hand and kissed her wrist. Since Davis had shown up, Rafe had tried to keep the affection down to a minimum. He hated it. He missed threading his fingers through hers and pulling her in for a kiss when the urge hit. He missed the easy way they'd talked and how he'd finally remembered who he was when he was with her.

She lifted her head from his shoulder and peered at him. He kissed her palm, closed his eyes, and pressed her hand to his cheek. Why couldn't life just be simple for once? He'd found his princess and swept her off her feet. Wasn't this where his happily ever after was supposed to happen?

Maybe all those movies Eva forced him to watch were nothing but lies. No, otherwise Zeke and Sosimo wouldn't have gotten their perfect ending. Even Jake had found true love. Rafe's heart clenched. More than likely the problem lay with him. He pressed her hand more firmly against his cheek. He wasn't prince material.

Plucky sidekick, maybe, but not the hero. His inability to track Piper's stalker proved that.

"Don't you dare, Rafe Malone." Piper's voice cracked.

Rafe's heart splintered. He was hurting her again. She flexed her fingers through his beard. He pushed aside his cowardice and opened his eyes.

He expected worry to be pulling at her features. Her bright red cheeks and blazing eyes caught him off guard and quickened his pulse. Good thing she wasn't a mythical goddess, otherwise she'd be striking people down with her sheer force. Where had this Piper been hiding?

"Don't you even dare believe anything my creep of a brother has said."

"Piper." He averted his eyes down the beach.

"No, Rafe, you listen to me. After years of dreaming and hoping, I've finally gotten your attention." She placed her other hand on his cheek and forced him to look at her. "You make me feel alive and beautiful for the first time in my life. You make me want to chase after my dreams—mine, not anyone else's. I'm marrying you, Rafe Malone. We're going to fill our house with love and babies. All my life I've prayed to be a mom and wife, just like my mother. Since I was fourteen, you've been the one walking through the door each evening in my dreams."

She leaned forward and pressed trembling lips to his. Everything faded but her and her crazy words that stalled his breath and set his skin tingling in the ocean breeze. He wanted her dream more than anything he'd ever wanted in his entire life.

Her breath stuttered and tangled with his. He caught

it, swallowing her anger and pain, and kissed her in return. The desire to nestle their children against his side while he read them stories warmed his gut. The image of her sharing his life with him until they were old and gray burned hot under his skin.

She pulled away, her chin set and raised stubbornly. "I'm marrying you. I don't care what that stupid brother of mine thinks."

A thousand tropical birds flapped in his stomach. He had to tell her before he exploded. "I—"

"You don't care what I think." Davis's sharp words sliced through the air and burst the moment to shreds.

Piper's newly tanned face paled, and she swallowed so hard Rafe heard it. "Davis, I—"

"I have always protected you. Always wanted what's best for you." Davis's nostrils flared, and Piper scrambled off the hammock.

Rafe stood, keeping his eyes on Davis. Rafe crossed his arms to hold back from taking a swing at Davis's face. His best friend's neck corded as he steamed where he'd stopped at the edge of the cabana.

"Davis, please, calm down." Piper took a step toward her brother, her hands held out in front of her.

"I want more for you than this guy." Davis motioned his hands wide. "You don't know the things he's done."

Rafe's face tingled and heated with the words. Denial sprang up his throat, but he couldn't push it past the boulders lodged there. How could he? Davis spoke the truth.

"I don't care." Piper's voice was firm and without

hesitation. "If God forgets Rafe's past as far as the east is from the west, why should it matter to me?"

Davis laughed, the sound razor-edged. "You're so naïve. You can't trust him. You can't trust anyone."

"It's you I can't trust." Piper's raised voice cracked. "You're the one breaking my heart!"

"Piper." Rafe placed a hand on her back.

He should take her back up to the house and let Davis cool off. Rafe had never seen Davis this mad before. He looked about to implode, and Rafe didn't want Piper anywhere near him when it happened.

"No." Piper stepped forward, and Davis clenched his fists. "Rafe has always been there for you, and he's never let me down."

"Hasn't he? What about the years you spent pining away for him, and he didn't have a clue?" His voice bit, causing Piper's shoulders to flinch. "You didn't think I noticed your pathetic crush, but I did. The only reason he's suddenly interested in you is because he doesn't have his video games to play with."

"You're wrong." Piper took a step back.

"Besides, why worry about missing a video game, when he has you crawling into his bed? You're just a temper—"

Rafe swung his arm hard, connecting with Davis's cheek and snapping his so-called best friend's head sideways. How dare he talk to Piper like that? He could be mad at Rafe all he wanted, but Rafe wouldn't stand there and let Davis say those things about Piper.

Davis growled and rammed his head into Rafe's gut. The stench of alcohol covered Rafe as he stumbled backward and landed on the hammock. Time slowed as the hammock swung their clamoring bodies before snapping and crashing to the ground. Rafe bucked his hips, but Davis clung tight. Davis's fist connected with Rafe's chin. His teeth knocked together, and he tasted blood. Rafe blocked Davis's next punch and slammed one of his own into Davis's head, knocking him off balance.

Rafe pushed Davis off and scrambled to his feet just in time to see Piper running down the beach. "Piper!"

She stumbled, but gained her feet and turned into the island foliage. Rafe had to find her. Had to make sure she was okay.

Davis's body struck Rafe's back. Rafe pivoted, tripping Davis, who was clumsy with rage, and threw him to the ground.

Rafe stepped back and held his hands in front of him in surrender. "What's your problem?" His chest heaved for air.

"You are." Davis staggered to his feet, wiping blood from his nose as he swayed.

"Davis," Rafe's voice cracked and he let his arms drop. "I'm not your enemy, man. You're ..." He looked out to the ocean to try to control the emotion stinging his eyes. He wiped his cheek with the back of his hand and returned his focus to Davis. "You're my best friend. I promise you. I fought what's going on between Piper and me. I did." He swallowed as a humorless laugh blew from his nose. "I know better than you I don't deserve her. I've screwed up in the past, but you know me. I'd die before I hurt her, man. She's my heart. I'm a better man, a better person because of her."

"It won't last, and you know it."

Rafe rubbed his hand across his chest and hung his head. His heart pounded hard against his ribs. How could he get Davis to understand? Rafe sniffed as tears dropped from his nose and splashed onto the decking.

Rafe wiped blood from his mouth. He couldn't talk to Davis when he was like this. Might never be able to talk to his best friend again. Rafe turned his back on the one person he'd always trusted and walked away.

NINETEEN

"IDIOTS. Rolling around like a couple of children," Piper muttered as she stomped through trees.

Did Davis really think she did what he said? The pain jabbed at her heart again, and she doubled over. How could he say something so horrid to her? How could he think so low of Rafe?

Her chest heated again, pushing the pain to a dull pulse. She spun back toward the beach. He thought he could cut her down like that? She had a few of her own cannons she could blast his way. She stopped short, shook her head, then went back the way she had originally been heading.

She didn't want to wound Davis. He obviously hurt enough already. She slowed her pace. He never would've said such things to her if something wasn't tormenting him. What if he truly was against her and Rafe being together?

She froze.

What if Rafe listened?

She'd seen the doubt in the faraway look in Rafe's eyes. When he'd pressed her hand against his cheek, she could feel his goodbye building between them. He hadn't reacted once to the horrid things Davis had said about Rafe. No, he'd flown into action after Davis's slashing comments turned to her. So, either Rafe believed what Davis said, or Rafe was trying not to rile Davis more.

From Rafe's monotone voice when he'd said her name and tried to lead her away from her brother, she'd bet her last dollar Rafe thought Davis spoke the truth that she and Rafe shouldn't be together. The heat rose in her cheeks again and the shard in her heart twisted more firmly in place. She wanted Rafe to forget his past, or at least not let it strangle him anymore.

She tipped her head back as she meandered through the trees. The melodic singing of the birds helped her focus through the emotions that had overwhelmed her rationale. She had a lifetime to help Rafe slay his demons. Shoot. She'd take up the sword herself until he found the strength to do it.

She could do the same for Davis as well. She'd spent the last ten years praying for both their safety during their physical battles while in the Army. Now, the war they both fought, while spiritual, raged just as brutal and could destroy every good thing Rafe and Davis had in their lives.

She glanced around at the coconut trees and tropical brush, pushing her shoulders back as her spirit filled with purpose. She'd have to pray for strength. Being on the front lines of this battle was bound to hurt, especially if Rafe's doubt grew and Davis continued to spew nastiness. Yet, she'd spent enough time hiding in a foxhole, thinking her passive involvement in life would satisfy.

The birds' song morphed to chaotic squawking. The sound scraped down her spine like fingernails on a chalkboard. The enemy already pushed against her newfound determination. The clamoring increased with the sudden flapping of a hundred wings.

She wrapped her arms around herself and narrowed her eyes. "Devil, you better just move on. Your intimidation won't work here."

Hard arms clamped around her, pinning hers to her body.

"Wanna bet?" A voice filled with menace bubbled acid in her stomach.

She whimpered, the sound hardly registering over the thrashing of her heart in her ears. Her mouth opened as a primal scream crawled up her throat. Pain spiked through the back of her head, crumpling her knees beneath her.

Rafe glanced at his watch as he paced in front of the living room window. His stomach attempted to crawl out of his throat. There was no reason for the anxiety, but it persisted to claw its way up with each second that passed.

Was he worried she wouldn't forgive him? He pushed his hand through his hair and shook his head. No, that wasn't it.

"Dude, you wear out Zeke's floor, and he won't be happy." Derrick flipped the page of his Louis L'Amour book without looking up. "What's got your boxers all in a bunch?"

"It's Piper."

"I've only known her a week, and even I know she'll forgive you two bozos for decking it out." Derrick snorted. "My bet is she comes back in and is ready to kiss all your boo-boos better."

"Nah, it's not that." Rafe stopped, the building in his chest almost overpowering all other thought. "Something's not right."

He took off at a run for the door. Derrick tossed the book aside and vaulted from the couch to follow. Rafe had to find Piper and find her now.

"What's wrong?" Davis called from the hallway, but Rafe didn't have time to answer.

"Piper." Derrick's voice strained behind Rafe as he sprinted down the stairs to the cabana.

Rafe rushed up the beach, pushing as hard as he could. He veered into the foliage where she had turned and focused on the slight dips in the sand. He stumbled to a stop as the footprints crisscrossed over themselves. He studied them, trying to figure out their direction. Davis and Derrick arrived, sucking air as their chests heaved.

"Still fast as lightning." Davis shook his head and put his hands around his mouth. "Piper!"

Rafe signaled for them to fan out and to spread in the direction she had run. Why wasn't she answering? Rafe's gut bubbled with the burning acid of fear.

"Rafe!" Derrick's call pulled Rafe's attention.

He pushed through the brush and stopped short by

Derrick as he crouched where he surveyed the ground. Rafe hated tracking in loose sand where prints shifted and filled with the slightest disturbance. Davis barreled through the leaves on the opposite side. He gave Rafe a wide-eyed look that had to mirror his own.

"There was someone else with her." Derrick's deep voice steeled.

Rafe swallowed the bile that filled his throat. He snapped his head to the ground and searched for what had happened.

"Here." Davis pointed and took off through the palms across the island away from the house.

Rafe followed, not allowing the sight of drag marks through the sand to freeze him. He stumbled out of the brush onto the empty beach. A large divot in the sand and the marks of a recently moored boat were the only indication someone had been there.

"Piper!" Davis's anguished yell as he fell to his knees raised all the hairs on Rafe's neck.

He'd failed her.

Vomit spewed out of his mouth as he doubled over. How had they been found? *God, please clear my mind.*

Peace settled over Rafe, though his skin still buzzed. He wanted to run, to do anything that would get Piper back to him, but he stilled. He bowed his head and clenched his fists at his side, willing his mind to slow enough to reveal what eluded him.

Cold wind whipped against his face, causing him to shiver and reminding him of the blizzard that had assaulted the ranch. He thought of his and Piper's trip to the store, and how the stalker had left her that rose. He furrowed his forehead. No one could've sat in that storm for days waiting for them to leave. If the freezing temperatures hadn't driven the sicko in, the snowplows would have buried his vehicle in the snow when they'd cleaned the roads that morning.

Which meant ...

Rafe's head snapped up, and he bolted back to the house.

"What do you have?" Derrick's voice hollered after Rafe.

"Tracker!"

Why hadn't he thought of it before? If the guy hadn't been stalking the house, he had somehow put a tracker on Piper. Rafe wanted Davis to take another swing at his head for being so stupid. He'd been so focused on tracking the messages Piper had received, he never thought about how the stalker kept finding her.

He banged into the house and shot to her room. The space smelled of her. The rich scent that normally pooled heat in his stomach stabbed pain through his heart. Would he ever bury his face in her hair and breathe her in again? Had he lost her before he ever got to tell her he loved her? He longed to tell her that her dream of marriage filled him with so much hope he wanted to cry.

He pushed the doubt aside and focused. All that mattered was Piper. All other thoughts could wait.

He crossed to her dresser and snatched her purse. The contents tumbled onto the bed just as Derrick's and Davis's thundering steps echoed down the hall.

The instant they stepped in the room, Rafe shot

orders. "Search her stuff. The guy put a tracker on her somehow."

Rafe rifled through lipstick, gum, and gluten-free snacks. He turned the purse inside-out and searched all the seams. When he came up empty, he scoured the items again, opening packages and wrappers. Pulling the items out of her wallet, a flash of shiny on a business card caught his eye. White-hot anger rushed up his neck as he lifted it to examine it, his eyes widening at what this meant.

TWENTY

PIPER STIRRED as a bird squawked obnoxiously out her window. Stupid tropical birds. Didn't they know it was rude to wake people up? Maybe she could drown them out if she pressed the other pillow over her ear.

She went to roll over, and pain spiked through her skull. She moved her hands to cup her head, but something tight and biting stopped them. Her eyes flew open and her heart pounded. She squinted as blinding light exploded in her head, making her sick to her stomach.

She tried moving her legs and arms, but they wouldn't budge. Her breath rasped fast, and she willed it to slow before she passed out. She opened one eye carefully, then the other. A scream built in her throat as her bound hands and feet filled her vision, but she pushed it down. She had to keep her wits. Maybe she could figure out how to escape.

She glanced around the room, pushing past the pain in her head, and sat up in the dingy bed. Her feet were bound together with zip ties and then tied to the brass footboard. The rope also connected her ankles to the zip ties wrapped around her wrists. She twisted her hands and feet, and the hard plastic cut into her bare skin.

Come on, Piper. Think. What had Davis drilled into her and Chloe's brains that one time he came home all geared up and forced survival school on them?

Assess your surroundings. Davis's voice filled her brain.

"Okay," she whispered hoarsely before squeezing her lips tight. She didn't want her captor to know she was awake.

She scanned the room again, taking in every corner. The furnishings were sparse, just a rickety table and chair pushed against the corrugated tin wall and a kitchen made of crates stacked on their sides with a slab of plywood laid on top for a counter. The wind rattled the metal siding and roof. The plastic covering the window fluttered violently.

If she could get her hands and feet free, she could easily get out the window. She focused on the zip ties on her wrists. Good. It wasn't handcuffs. She bent her head to her hands, took the end of the zip tie in-between her teeth, and pulled, tightening the binding as far as it would go. Lifting her hands as high as she could get them with the rope tied to her feet, she slammed her wrists down against her knees. She bit her lips to keep her whimper in as the plastic held and sliced her skin.

Please. This had to work. She adjusted her position, raised her hands high, then, with as much force as she could muster, brought her hands down, ramming the tie into her gut. The snap of the plastic sprung tears to her eyes, which she blinked away. She wasn't free yet.

Her heart picked up its beat, urging her to hurry. She wouldn't be able to do the same thing with her legs without making a ton of noise. She untied the rope, then felt in her hair. She huffed out a shaky breath and smiled when her finger connected with the bobby pin. She yanked it out, popped the plastic tip off the end, then shoved the metal into the connector on the zip tie.

She just needed to disrupt the teeth from gripping the plastic. Her hands shook and grew slick with blood that ran down her wrists from where the ties had cut. She wiped her hands on the bedding and tried again. As she pulled against the tie, she felt it give and her feet fell apart as the zip tie broke open.

Relief ballooned so light she could've floated out of the shack. Since that wasn't possible, she tiptoed to the chair, picked it up as silently as she could, and placed it under the window. Would the metal hold her or fold under her weight? What would she find when she got to the other side?

It didn't matter. She didn't dare try the door, and she couldn't stay here. Sketchy window it was. She climbed up onto the chair, ripped the plastic off the window, and tested her body on the bottom of the opening. The metal groaned, but just a little. The opening was small though, and there wasn't any way for her to hold on. She'd have to lead with her head and fall out to escape.

She poked her head out, looking left and right. Sand and palm trees greeted her. Her stomach dropped to her toes. She was hoping for people, someone she might get help from. She squared her shoulders. She didn't need help. She could get free and figure the next step later.

Glancing down, she assessed that the drop wouldn't be far and the sand would cushion the landing. The wind whipped her hair in front of her face and made her shiver. Her eyes widened at the sinister dark clouds building on the horizon. She needed to get out and find a place to hole up fast.

She leaned farther out, cringing as the metal groaned beneath her and sliced into her belly. She tucked her head just as the sound of the door opening scraped against the planked floor.

"No!" A bellow behind her had her letting herself fall forward.

The air whooshed out of her as she thudded onto the sand. *Move. Hurry.* She scrambled, trying to get to her knees when a roar sounded through the thin metal, chilling her more than the cold wind beating against her skin. She pushed to her feet just as something slammed into her back, throwing her to the ground.

She threw her elbow backward as hard as she could. The crunch of bone on bone and the enraged curse gave her little satisfaction as her assailant shoved her face into the sand. She flailed her arms, scratching at the hand gripping her hair. She couldn't breathe—needed air. She didn't want to die here.

Doubling her strength, she threw her arm back toward her attacker. When it connected and knocked him off-balance, she used the momentum to twist, throwing a handful of sand toward his face. She didn't stop to see if it worked, just got to her feet and took her first glorious step to freedom.

Arms wrapped around her ankles, and she went down hard, smacking her head against the metal shack. She kicked her feet and threw her fists. Anything she could think of to get free. Strong legs wrapped around hers and the weight of her attacker pressed against her torso, pinning her arms in his hands.

"No." She shook her head as her captor's face fully registered. "No, not you."

"Hello, Piper."

Eyes that had always been kind hardened in anger as he lifted his fist and slammed it against her temple. Her heart sank as everything went black.

TWENTY-ONE

"ELIAS DRAKE." Rafe dashed out of the room toward the office, anger building hot in his chest.

"The drummer?" Derrick called after him.

Rafe stalked into the office and jammed the keys on his keyboard to pull up his computer programs. While they booted up, he twisted the sophisticated tracking device masked as a business card in his hand. "I think he's been stalking Piper for a while."

Derrick's eyes narrowed as he reached out and grabbed the tracker. "This is some sophisticated tech."

Rafe nodded, glancing at his computer. Why was it taking so long for it to load? He paced to the window and back as Davis came into the small space.

"D, man, think you can call up Zeke and get someone on my computers back home? We need to see what I missed when I did a background check on the band. With this computer, I won't be able to do everything here."

"On it." Derrick handed Davis the card, reached into

his pocket, and pulled out his phone as he headed out of the office.

Rafe's computer beeped at him, indicating that the system was up and running. He crashed into the chair and raced his fingers over the keyboard. He'd been wasting time running down rabbit trails that led to nowhere. A sharp pain speared up his cheek where he clenched his jaw. How could he have possibly missed all of this?

He shook off the shame and anger. Whining about it wouldn't save Piper. Now that he knew how the creep was keeping her in his sights, Rafe could trace the tracker back to its source. Just a little trick he picked up in special ops school of taking down the bad guys.

"Can you find her?" Davis leaned against the wall, his face tight with worry.

"Yeah. It's not easy, but I should be able to figure out where the device was bouncing to," Rafe answered as he typed code into the program. He held out his hand to Davis, who placed the card in Rafe's palm.

"How long will it take?"

"Not sure. Could be a few minutes. Could be a few hours." Rafe tried not to let the question build anxiety in his throat.

"Well, hurry up." Davis pushed off the wall and moved toward the window.

Rafe scowled as he followed Davis's gaze. He didn't need the extra pressure clogging his brain and making him miss something. Ice chilled his hands as he looked past Davis. The building storm on the horizon registered in his brain.

"Davis, get everything ready. There's gear in the basement, the farthest door on the north side. We'll take the speedboat." Rafe turned back to the screen with renewed urgency. "At least with a storm brewing, he won't be able to fly."

"On it." Davis dashed out of the room, his pounding footsteps fading to silence.

The wind beat against the window, mocking Rafe's lack of foresight. They could have gotten this jerk days ago if Rafe hadn't had tunnel vision. He jammed the return key and sat back as the program began cycling.

He pressed the heel of his hands against his eyes. He thought back to the few instances the drummer had even said anything. Rafe hadn't picked up on vibes from him when they'd all come to the house. Of course, Rafe's desire to rip Chet, the over-amorous guitarist's fingers off might have clouded his reasoning. Then when Chet had pushed too far in New York, Elias had seemed like a concerned friend, not a psycho-stalker.

Derrick stomped into the room, pulling on a tactical jacket. "Dude, the reason you didn't find anything is because there's nothing there." He rolled his shoulders, like he needed to contain his energy from bursting. "He's just been bouncing from place to place, picking up gigs since he got out of high school."

Rafe stood and paced to the window, not able to sit still any longer. "What about his parents?"

"Mom's a housewife. Dad's some bigwig professor at MIT." Derrick ran a hand over his shaved head. "If he hurts our Piper ..."

Rafe wouldn't be able to find forgiveness from his sins

if Elias hurt Piper. The things Rafe would do to the man would buy Rafe a one-way ticket to hell. If Elias hurt Piper, or worse—Rafe shook his head. He couldn't let that thought in.

Rafe grabbed onto the one bit of information that gave any indication how Elias could accomplish what he'd done. "What did his dad teach?"

"He's the head of the Electrical Engineering and Computer Science department." Derrick crossed his arms, never one to be interested too much in brains, as much as brawn. He never understood why someone would want to sit in front of a computer all day when they could be outside using their muscles.

"So, Elias must've learned to program from his dad." Rafe turned to the clouds that had darkened to almost black. "His dad, the freaking head of computer science at MIT."

Rafe's ribs closed in on his lungs, making it difficult to breathe. This guy wasn't just some clown who tinkered with computers on the weekends. What if Elias somehow hid his trail? What if Rafe couldn't piggyback on the signal and track the tracker?

Rafe's head spun, and he placed his hand on the glass to steady himself. What if he never found Piper? A lancing pain jabbed in his stomach and sliced up to his heart. There wouldn't be life without her.

TWENTY-TWO

"WELL, it looks like we're stuck here for a while." Elias's words snaked into Piper's head as she groaned in pain.

She'd tried to ignore Elias. How could it be him? He'd hardly ever talked to her after he'd first approached her while Chloe was playing in a local bar. He hadn't gushed or built himself up when he asked about joining Chloe's band. He'd simply handed her his business card and explained that he'd been watching for a while and wanted to be a part of what was sure to be a success. She shivered at the memory. Just how long had he been watching?

Her head pounded like the stormy waves against the shore. He'd tied her arms to the headboard, stretching them above her head and making her muscles burn. Her body hurt in so many places she'd stopped cataloging the pain.

The sound of tape ripping popped her eyes open. Elias tore a piece of duct tape from the roll with his teeth and placed it on the plastic covering the window. He smiled over at her. The look slithered a thousand snakes down her spine.

"Hopefully that keeps the storm out. It's supposed to be a doozy. Possibly turn into a hurricane." Elias chuckled, looking embarrassed. "I guess it would be a typhoon since we're in the South Pacific."

She didn't care one flying fig what the weather was called. The easy conversation churned her stomach. If she timed it right, maybe she could vomit on him. She couldn't get untied the way she was, but she could still make things miserable for him.

She stared at the dried blood under his nose and on his chin. Her lip lifted in a smile that probably bordered on a sneer. She hoped his broken nose pounded pain into his skull. Was it sinful to feel satisfaction at causing him even a little hurt? She closed her eyes so she couldn't see him. She didn't care if it was or not. If she got the chance, she'd smash his nose again, break other bones as well.

"Why don't we get you cleaned up?" Something in Elias's tone raised the hair on her neck.

"I'm fine." She choked out.

"No, baby. You cut yourself on the window ledge." His use of a nickname made her shiver. "I don't want it to get infected."

"How ... how did you find us?" Maybe if she kept him talking, he wouldn't touch her.

He shrugged as he wet a washrag with water from a bottle, scrubbed the blood off of his face, and rinsed the rag out. "Easy. I just followed the tracking device."

"Tracking device? How ... when ..."

"You're adorable when you're confused." His normal

expression, like a doting boyfriend, had her head spinning.

He was supposed to be harmless. He'd always been just the guy who showed up for practice and didn't say much. Even when they'd all hang out or traveled for a gig, he kept to himself, mostly reading a book or watching funny videos on the internet. She'd sat next to him unknown hours, watching clips he'd show her and enjoying companionable silence. He'd never given her a clue he liked her ... especially to this extreme.

"I gave you the tracking device months ago."

"Gave me?" Her stomach quivered.

"Yeah. I couldn't believe you kept my business card all this time." Elias shook his head as he ran his hand through his hair. "I mean, I knew it was a gamble. Figured I'd have to get another one on you somehow, but you kept it."

He smiled at her like she'd just given him a puppy and told him he'd won a million dollars. She shivered. He'd been keeping tabs on her that long? Had known where she was every moment of every day for months?

"How do you even know how to do that kind of stuff?"

"Genes, I guess. My dad's a computer genius. I started messing with them when I was like two. Watched a spy movie once and became fascinated with the gadgets they used." He wrung out the rag, stepped close, and kneeled in front of her stomach. "I've made quite a little fortune selling my tracking devices on the black market. Gives me the ability to follow my dream of music. Let me find you."

As he pulled up the hem to her shirt and reached the cloth to her stomach, she caved away from him. The bindings kept her from going far. She couldn't have him touching her. A whimper escaped as his eyebrows furrowed. She swallowed next when he licked his lips and his skin flushed. She needed to be strong and figure out how to get out of this. How to fight.

"I know this will sting, my love, but it has to be done. Then, after the storm, we'll leave for my place I've got hidden away where we can be together, just the two of us, forever."

The words steeled her spine and heated her chest in anger.

He didn't love her.

Didn't know what that word meant.

Love didn't slink behind corners and peek through windows. Love didn't force and hurt for one's own pleasure. Love strengthened you, like Rafe's had done for her. It healed and helped, like hers had for Rafe. She refused to let Elias force her to do anything. She'd fight with all she had until he got sick of her and left her to die. The thought of death iced through her stomach, but the thought of life without Rafe would be an endless blizzard.

Yet, what could she do tied like she was? She looked at Elias's face, and her lips pressed tight together. She'd gotten him good when she'd whacked him with her elbow. One eyebrow lifted and her mouth turned up slightly at the corner. Served him right.

"Elias?" Her voice shook as she said his name.

He tore his gaze from her exposed stomach, a crease slashing down his forehead. "What?"

Piper cleared her throat. "Please, let me go."

He sat up straighter. "No."

She bit her bottom lip, and his gaze darted to her mouth. His eyes widened, and he rubbed the back of his hand across his mouth. She really was going to throw up.

"Piper." His voice dipped low and gravelly.

She looked away so she wouldn't have to see his face. She pushed herself toward the headboard so her arms bent in front of her face. It didn't give her much movement, but hopefully it'd be enough if he tried something.

She took a deep breath. His gaze moved to her chest, and her stomach twisted. *Please, just leave me alone.*

"I'd ... I'd like to kiss you, see if my daydreams were right or not." His voice trembled with anticipation.

She shook her head. His breath came out fast as he scrambled to kneel in front of her. With a shaking hand, he brushed away the hair that had fallen across her cheek. Goosebumps spread across her skin, and she hid her face in disgust.

He forced her face toward him and rubbed his thumb over her bottom lip. "I've been dreaming about this for months."

She pressed her lips together. He leaned toward her, his hand pushing into her hair. He groaned low in his throat when he was an inch away. The sound hardened her resolve to fight.

She clamped her elbows around his head and bit down on his nose. Salty blood gushed in her mouth, but she held on. She cringed at his anguished squeal. His fingers ripping at her hair and his cursing bolstered her to push past the remorse she felt for hurting him. How could she feel guilty after all that he'd done?

His punch to the side of her face caused her to gasp and let go of his nose. He stumbled backward, falling against the table. He touched shaking hands to his face and stared at his blood-covered fingers. His neck corded as he looked at her. She spit the blood from her mouth and lifted her chin.

His lips pulled back to bare bloodied teeth. He tipped his head back and released a scream so primal her muscles convulsed and tears sprang to her eyes. As he barreled toward her, she readied to lift her legs and defend herself.

TWENTY-THREE

RAFE JUMPED ONTO THE BEACH, his legs wobbling underneath him after the wild ride through stormy waters. He steeled them and took off for the shack on the beach. He'd found her faster than he'd ever hoped.

The tiny island, not even ten klicks from Zeke's, had been easy enough to locate, even in the nasty weather. He'd wanted to dive into the churning sea and swim to her the instant he saw the small shanty tucked in the palm trees. He suppressed the urge, barely.

He dashed up the beach, not waiting for Davis or Derrick. The storm drove hard on his face. It pushed against him as if wanting to keep him from Piper. At least it would hide their approach. The wind screeched, standing all his hairs on end. They'd have to leave fast, or they might have to weather the storm here.

Fifty feet. Fifty feet and then he'd have her safely in his arms. A primal howl hit him and dropped a boulder of ice into his stomach. *Piper!*

He pushed harder.

Stretched his stride longer.

Another roar had his fingers going numb. He darted a glance behind him. Davis and Derrick struggled with mooring the boat against the beating of the building storm. Rafe wasn't waiting.

The door swung against the metal siding as Rafe kicked it open. His heartbeat pounded in his ears and vision tunneled to Piper on the bed with her legs wrapped around Elias's neck in a choke hold as he struck her in the thigh, attempting to loosen her hold. She had squeezed her eyes shut like she didn't want to watch what she was having to do.

Rafe lunged into the room, grabbed Elias's hand as he swung it for another punch, and threw him across the small space.

Piper's eyes flew open. "Rafe."

Her rigid body sagged into the filthy bed. His hands shook as he reached for Piper. Blood covered her head and body.

"Piper?" He touched her shoulder, and she sobbed.

His breath rushed out of him. She was alive. Now to get her out of here. He flipped his knife out and cut the ties on her wrists that had rubbed raw and were bleeding.

Scrambling sounded behind him and he turned to see Elias struggling to his feet with a knife in his hand. "She's mine."

Davis yelled from the door and rushed into the room. Rafe turned back to Piper as the sound of a fist impacting flesh filled the room. The clang of the knife skidding across the floor soon followed.

She had curled into a ball and covered her face with

her hand, another muffled sob choking out from behind her fingers. He wanted to pull her into his arms and bawl right along with her. The amount of blood covering her and the need to see to her injuries pushed the feeling aside.

"Oh, Piper." He slid his hand along her arm. "Where are you hurt?"

"Not mine." Her words sagged his body in to the floor. "Elias."

He glanced back to where Davis beat a cowering Elias. "Come on. We need to get you out of here."

Her eyes widened as she glanced around him toward the scuffle. "Davis, no."

She winced as she tried to get off the bed. Rafe placed an arm around her, but she pushed him away.

"Please, stop him." Piper's pleading burned hot in his stomach.

Rafe didn't want to stop Davis. He would be fine with his friend beating the sicko to a pulp. Piper went to stand and wobbled back to the ground.

"Please." She sobbed.

Rafe stood just as Derrick charged into the shack.

"We have a problem. The storm's too big to keep the boat moored," Derrick rushed out between breaths.

Rafe pointed to Davis with his chin. "Get him."

Derrick clapped Davis on the shoulder and pulled him away from Elias. "He's done, man."

Davis shook off Derrick and lunged for Elias.

"Davis, no," Piper hollered, stumbling toward him.

Davis's shoulders and chest rose and fell as he sucked

in air. His face contorted in anguish when he looked at Piper.

"Please, let's just go." Piper grabbed onto Rafe's arm. "I want to go."

Rafe scooped her into his arms and stomped out of the shanty. Derrick could deal with Davis and Elias. He was getting Piper to the boat.

The boat bobbed precariously in the ocean. The rope tying it to the shore stretched to its max. He waded into the raging water and lifted her carefully over the boat's side. She was crawling to the seat at the back of the boat when he pulled himself in.

He scooped her up and settled her on his lap. Her sobs as she buried her face into his neck ripped his heart apart. Derrick came out of the shack with Elias thrown over his shoulder. Elias wouldn't be able to hurt Piper again. Rafe would make sure of that.

He closed his lids against the stinging in his eyes and tightened his arms around Piper. She gripped his shirt in her hand and curled her body around his as if worried he'd disappear. Not a chance. He wasn't ever letting her go again.

TWENTY-FOUR

BACK AT THE BEACH HOUSE, Piper stared at
herself in the mirror of her bathroom. She shouldn't have
wiped the steam off the smooth glass. Shouldn't have
looked, but just crawled into bed. She'd had to see what
she looked like—had to pile more heartache on to the day.

The instant her gaze hit the angry cut across her forehead, the last few hours came rushing in, bombarding her
with fear and pain. She tore her eyes from the ugly cut
and stared herself down in the mirror. She didn't have to
let the fear win.

"You fought." Her whisper wasn't very convincing.

It hadn't been a smart move, biting Elias like she had.
All it'd done was enrage him. But she couldn't just let
him do what he had wanted, either.

A shiver raced up her skin still hot from the long
shower.

"Piper, honey, are you okay?" Rafe's question through
the closed door jolted her.

"Yeah." She closed her eyes to the tremble in her voice. She wasn't okay, not by far.

She heard a soft thunk against the door, and when he spoke next, the clear sound made her wonder if his head leaned against the wood. "I need ..." He cleared his throat. "I need to look at your cuts. I ... I don't want them to get infected."

Why was she so hesitant to leave this room? She wanted Rafe, wanted his arms around her, telling her everything was okay. Yet, Elias was out there somewhere in the house. *Come on, Piper.* She shook her head. How could she fly back to the states with him in the plane when she couldn't muster enough courage to leave the bathroom?

Filling her lungs with air, though the motion hurt, she reached a shaking hand and turned the knob. Rafe straightened from where he leaned against the doorjamb. He'd showered and changed, but his hair stuck out in all directions. His eyebrows pinched together as he reached for her hand.

He swallowed and looked away from her. "Come on. Let me take a peek at those two cuts."

Her legs trembled as he pulled her into the bedroom. Would she ever feel stable again, or would her insides always resemble pudding? Her knees gave out as she neared the bed, and she flopped more than sat on the edge of it.

Rafe kneeled before her and cleaned the wound on her head with peroxide. He cringed when she hissed and blew on the jagged cut like her mom had when she was little. The cut wasn't deep, but still made her stomach turn with pain.

He grabbed a bright blue glass jar on the nightstand and twisted the lid off. "Mama J, Zeke's stepmom, made this healing balm." He dipped his fingers in it. They trembled as he stretched them toward her forehead. "She's always pushing this essential oil mumbo jumbo on us." His throat bobbed and his chuckle sounded forced. "Crazy stuff works."

The warm floral scent soothed Piper, so she breathed it in deeply. He poured more peroxide onto a cotton ball and reached toward her belly. With stiff fingers, she lifted her hem so he could tend to the ragged cut. The wound had stung so much when she'd washed it out in the shower, she'd almost thrown up. She steeled herself so she didn't toss her cookies in front of him.

"Oh, Piper." He groaned as he dabbed the peroxide over the cut and sniffed. "Maybe I should ... I think this ... this might need stitches."

"No." She jerked her hem down, the ointment stinging as it stuck to her shirt. "Not right now, please. Can we just let it be for a while?"

"Yeah, sure. I can stitch it in a little bit." He peeked at her face, his pained expression slicing through her before he lowered his head and focused on capping the jar. "I should probably—"

"Stay."

His shoulders slumped, and his head bowed until it rested on her knees. Why was he so upset? He'd found her, saved her when she thought all was lost. She pushed her fingers through his hair, and his hands fisted into the loose fabric of her pants.

"I'm so sorry." His raw voice made her throat burn with tears.

"It's not your—"

"It is." His voice cracked. "I should have thought of the tracker sooner. Should have—he could've killed you. If we hadn't gotten there—"

"But you did. I shouldn't have gone off by myself." She rubbed her hand across her shoulder.

His eyes were red-rimmed when he peered up at her. "Did he—" He squeezed his eyes shut when his voice gave out.

"No. I think I lost my appeal when I tried to bite off his nose." She forced out a breath that was half laugh, half sob. "I ... I don't want to talk about it right now. I just ... I need you to hold me."

He slid his hand up her arm and cupped her neck, his thumb rubbing along her jaw. "Piper, I'll hold you the rest of my life if you let me. I don't think I'll ever be able to let you go again."

Her smile trembled as her eyes filled with tears. "That's good. I don't want you to let me go, either."

He leaned forward and kissed her lightly on the lips. "Scoot on up there."

She moved to the center of the bed as he crawled up with her. He stretched out on the comforter and pulled her so her head lay on his chest. His heart beat loudly against her ear, calming her with each steady thump. Her eyes stung, but she blinked the moisture away. She didn't want to focus on the terror she'd felt.

She wanted to relish Rafe's words and bottle up the strength she gained from being close to him. How could one day hold such intense fear and joy at the same time?

Rafe ran his hand softly up and down her arm draped across his chest. His other arm anchored her tightly to his side. Just possibly, if he stayed this close the entire way home, she could face that long plane ride. Could handle being in the same space as her nightmare without crumbling into a ball of fear. How could she have been so brave when Elias had her tied to that bed, but the very thought of him now made every part of her quiver?

"Hey, Pipstick." Davis's voice and knock on the doorjamb caused her to jump.

Rafe's hands tightened on her. "Shh, I've got you." His whisper was so soft she barely heard it.

"Are you okay?" Davis came into the bedroom, his hands wringing before him.

His eyes were bloodshot, like he'd been crying. She'd never seen him so hesitant before. Never seen him so strung out with emotion, even after their parents died. She sat up, and Rafe mirrored the motion, wrapping his arm around her back.

"I will be ... eventually. Thanks to you and Rafe and Derrick."

Davis's shoulders slumped as he nodded and gazed out the window. "About what I said earlier. I'm sorry. I've been a total jerk this entire time, taking my issues out on you two." He turned his eyes back to her. "I'm happy this numskull wised up. I can't think of a better man for you, Piper."

Rafe kissed her on the head. "Thanks, man." His voice cracked, and he cleared his throat.

Piper leaned toward Davis, pain jumping through her bruised muscles. "Can I get a hug?"

He sat on the edge of the bed and pulled her in. His strong arms wrapped around her hurt her sore body, but she held on just as tight. Here was the big brother who'd championed her growing up.

"I'm so sorry," he whispered into her hair.

"I forgive you, Davis." She squeezed him harder. "And I'm here for you, whatever I can do to help with what you're going through."

"We're both here for you, man." Rafe clapped Davis on the shoulder as he rubbed his other hand up and down Piper's back.

Davis sniffed, wiped his eyes across her shoulder, then sat up. "It's good to be back with family."

Piper smiled and kissed him on the cheek. She'd missed her brother so much. Davis took her hand and squeezed. Her heart jumped at his bruised knuckles, crashing the happiness that had bubbled up back down.

Davis sighed. "Listen, Derrick and I have decided we're going to take Elias back to the states, then come back to get you two."

Her body slumped back into Rafe's, and her throat ached. She wouldn't have to see Elias. Wouldn't have to sit in the same space as him. She nodded, the relief so thick it bottled up her voice.

"We've got a pocket clearing in the storm, so we're going to head out as soon as it's safe." Davis peeked out the window and squinted.

She glanced at his knuckles again, the memory of Elias's broken and bloodied body assaulting her brain. "Is he ... is he okay?"

Davis's eyebrows squished together as he turned back to her. "Elias?"

She nodded.

"Better than he deserves to be." Davis's jaw clenched.

"Davis?"

"He'll live."

Was it relief or vengefulness that warmed her chest and stung her eyes? *Oh Lord, help me not to grow bitter. Help me forgive.*

She took a deep breath to ease the tightness in her chest. "Thanks, Davis. I don't know if I could fly back with him."

"I didn't want you to have to." Davis patted her leg and stood. "All right. You two behave yourselves. We'll be back as soon as we can."

Piper buried her face into Rafe's chest as Davis strode from the room. The last of the remaining fear dissipated like morning fog on a sunny day. Rafe wrapped his arms gently around her and lay back down.

"Finally." He sighed. "I get you all to myself."

She snuggled closer to him as the worry and horror of the last few weeks leeched out of her. She closed her eyes and breathed in the floral scent of the healing ointment. As the thump of Rafe's heart and the light tapping of rain on the window filled her ears, she relaxed into the promise of a brighter tomorrow.

TWENTY-FIVE

RAFE TOSSED a palm branch into the pile of rubble on the beach as the sputtering of Emori's boat sounded over the joyful chirping of the island's birds. While the tropical storm still beat the area north of there, it had moved on from Zeke's island after a day and a half. The mess Rafe and Piper had spent the early afternoon cleaning was nothing to what people other places were in for as the storm built.

Piper threw an armful of palm branches onto the top of the pile and shielded her eyes from the sun as she peered toward the engine noise. A salty breeze pulled strands of hair from her braid out behind her, making Rafe jealous. He gave in to the temptation and ran his fingers over the soft braid. She turned her face to him and smiled.

"The wind made me do it." He put on the innocent expression he'd always used growing up.

She snorted and returned her gaze to the end of the beach. "I'm guessing it's Emori."

He inched closer and ran his hand down the length of her hair. If only he could take out the hair tie and thread his fingers through the silky strands. The coy look she gave him said she knew what he was thinking.

He cleared his throat. "Why do you think it's Emori?"

She shrugged. "My superior female instincts tell me the man couldn't wait to get out here and clean this place up. Everything about the grounds and the house scream that a perfectionist takes care of it. I figured he'd be here as soon as he set his own house to order, if not sooner."

"Your superior female instincts?"

"I may not be able to tell one motor from another, but I can spot another worrywart a mile away." She shrugged. "Let's go meet him, ease his anxiousness."

She pulled his hand away from her hair, threaded her fingers through his, and started toward the dock. He grinned. He loved it when she got bossy ... well, bossy for Piper, that is. It was like the attack had broken loose the last of her timidity.

She had hardly flinched when he'd stitched up the cut in her stomach, while his eyes had stung with tears so much he'd worried he'd sew her up crooked. When he'd told her he thought she should see someone to help her with any PTSD she might have from this ordeal, she agreed, but only if he'd see someone about his. Remembering the challenge she'd had in her eyes and the cute cocking of her eyebrow had his heart thumping hard in his chest all over again.

He wrapped his arm around her back and pulled her to a stop. When she tipped her head up in question, he captured her pretty pink lips in answer. She closed the distance between them and wrapped her arms around his neck. Everything he'd never realized he'd wanted had been right there in front of him all along.

The boat motor coughed to a stop, and Piper pulled away. Her cheeks were rosy with a blush, but the soft smile on her lips begged Rafe to kiss her again. The way she glanced at his lips said she wouldn't mind.

"Rafe, will you marry me?" Her soft question stopped his approach to her mouth.

He leaned back and stared into her eyes. He'd been burning to ask her the same question, but worried it was too soon. She broke eye contact and glanced over his shoulder.

He brought his hand to her chin and slid his thumb along her skin. "Yeah, Piper, I'll marry you, though you know that means you'll then be stuck with me, right?"

She beamed as she combed her fingers through his beard. "I've been stuck with you in my heart since I was fourteen." She took a deep breath and bit her lip. "What do you think about eloping?"

"Eloping?"

"Yeah." She leaned into him, spreading her palms on his chest. "I've been researching it, and we could get married in a day or two if we pulled the right strings."

When had she learned to read his mind?

"What about Davis and Chloe? Don't you want them at our wedding?" As much as he wanted his friends and family there for the wedding, he prayed she'd say no.

"Sure, part of me does." She leaned back and peered in his eyes. "But I've been waiting to marry you for years.

I don't want to wait any longer. Besides, we can have a big reception when we get back or something."

He pulled her up to him and ran his hands up her back. "Let's go say hello to Emori, then figure out the fastest way to get hitched."

He gave her a quick kiss, promising himself he'd take time to kiss her more thoroughly later, and turned to Emori. The groundskeeper ambled toward them with his son Timi following behind. Rafe forced himself to look at the boy. While Rafe still saw the similarities, his hands didn't slick with the sweat of guilt. His chest felt light and unconstrained with the hope of healing filling him.

He raised his hand and smiled. "Timi, what does a cloud wear under its raincoat?"

Timi's eyes widened and darted from Rafe to his dad. Emori gave his son an encouraging nod and patted him on the back.

"I ... I don't know." Timi's voice shook with nerves.

"Thunderwear."

White teeth flashed as the boy threw his head back and laughed. Rafe let his own joy free, the sound not ringing false in his ears anymore. Piper leaned in and kissed his cheek, and he squeezed her closer to his side. It had taken almost losing everything, but he'd discovered himself again.

Piper stared in the full-length mirror in the private villa Rafe had rented on the mainland. The ivory lace of her wedding dress hugged the length of her and made her tanned skin seem darker somehow. She turned to the side to peer at the open back that made her feel sexy and secretive since the lacy short sleeves suggested a more modest style.

She'd almost passed the dress up the day before when she'd been trying gowns on, even though she'd fallen in love with it the moment she'd slipped into it. The low-cut front had been a little too risqué, but the dressmaker had assured Piper she could adjust it. After being bold and asking Rafe to elope, she figured she should go for the dress that would make his eyes bulge out of his head and his hands itch to touch her.

Piper placed her hands on her scorching cheeks. Who was this woman that stared back at her in the mirror? She was daring and forward. The voice that had always urged Piper to stop being so shy was finally coming through to her in full force.

Piper lowered her hands and grinned into the mirror. She'd gone for her dreams, pushing aside all the doubts that had urged her to stay safe and had plunged in head first. Sure, she'd still help Chloe shoot for the stars, but that didn't mean Piper had to settle for remaining on solid ground. She had her own desires to go for.

"Miss, we're ready when you are." Anne, the friendly woman who had helped get the last-minute wedding arranged, entered from the patio door.

"Finally." Piper chuckled softly as she dashed to Anne.

"Your future is waiting on the other side of this glass." Anne motioned toward the beach visible through the sheer curtains.

"Thank you ... for everything," Piper said as she stepped through the doorway.

Shells of varying sizes lined a path to where Rafe waited with the local pastor. Rafe's shoulders relaxed under his loose white cotton shirt the moment he saw her. Her bare feet sunk in the warm sand as she made her way toward him.

Rafe took a hesitant step in her direction, then strode to her as if in a trance. She snorted a laugh and shook her head. He never was good at following directions.

He stopped before her, his Adam's apple bobbing as he took her in. "You look incredible." His voice broke and his eyes were bright with tears.

She closed the distance between them and pressed her lips to his. "Come on, handsome. Let's get hitched."

He laughed against her mouth and kissed her softly, before tucking her hand in his elbow and leading her to the amused pastor. Rafe's promise to love and cherish was strong and resolute, bringing tears to her eyes. As a gentle ocean breeze blew a salt-filled caress against her face, she became Mrs. Rafe Malone.

EPILOGUE

"I'M TELLING YOU, a joint wedding would be epic." Chloe's hands waved wildly and whacked Jake in the chest.

Derrick shook his head at Chloe's enthusiasm. She'd insisted that she and Jake go with Derrick and Davis to pick up Piper and Rafe, so now they all sat under the cabana, drinking cold drinks while Chloe tried to get her way. Jake sure had his hands full with that one. Derrick's mouth tweaked up on one side. Didn't seem like Jake minded at all.

"Chloe, everything with you is epic." Davis laughed.

Piper peeked over at Rafe, a secret smile passing between them. Those two had been acting strange since Derrick and the crew had landed earlier that morning. Derrick narrowed his eyes. Just what had happened the week they'd been gone?

Piper leaned into Rafe's side. "You know your mom will want to throw some big shindig and invite all her highfaluting friends. Reporters will swarm to get pictures of America's newest country darling and her hero fiancé getting hitched."

Chloe shook her head, her eyes big in her fairy-like face. "Oh no, I didn't think about that." She slumped against Jake's side. "That sounds horrid."

"The worst." Jake rubbed his hand up and down her arm, but a smile stretched across his face.

Derrick enjoyed seeing Jake happy again. His distance and the hurt that none of them could break through had been hard to handle the last two years. In reality, Jake's injury chilled Derrick to the core. He probably would've been a bigger mess than Jake if he didn't have a fully functioning body. Losing Derrick's best friend, Ethan, had ripped something vital out of his core, but losing a limb would have devastated him.

He shook off the thought, not wanting to dwell on how he'd failed to protect those he loved ... again. It'd taken him a long time to realize there had been nothing he could have done differently on that mission to save Ethan. It had been doomed from the start.

His gaze bounced between Rafe and Jake, glad to see their lives taking turns for the best. Derrick hadn't ever thought much about relationships past the flirting and stolen kisses while hanging out at the bars. He'd always had more pressing things to worry about, like rising in the rodeo ranks and then becoming the best soldier he could. Women had just been a nice diversion for an entertaining evening.

Now, however, with the ranks of his friends at the ranch falling in love around him left and right, the thought of his own next step in life rammed against his brain. Maybe it was time to think beyond the next physical challenge. Kiki Payne's bright blue eyes flashed before him, causing his forehead to furrow.

What the heck was that about? Sure, they'd become friends over the last few months as she adjusted to life out from under her parents' manipulation. That didn't mean there was more there than friendship. Besides, if he was going to get serious about moving on with life, he'd do better finding someone who enjoyed searching out adventures in the stockyards, not someone who got excited trading stocks behind a computer screen.

"I've got it." Chloe bobbed onto her knees. "What if we get married while we're here?"

"What? You're crazy." Davis laughed, shaking his head.

"People do it all the time, don't they? Have destination weddings in the tropics." Chloe glanced around at all of them, her eyes bright with excitement.

"Actually," Piper peeked up at Rafe, her cheeks turning bright red, "we can't have a joint wedding. Rafe and I already got married."

"What?" Chloe jumped from the couch, causing Jake to grunt as she pushed off of him. "You got married without us?"

Rafe stared down at Piper. "When Piper asked, I couldn't say no."

"You asked?" Davis's jaw dropped as he stared at his sister.

She shrugged. "I wasn't going to spend another moment daydreaming about marrying him if I didn't have to. Are you mad we didn't wait?"

Davis's forehead scrunched before it smoothed. "As long as you're happy, I'm happy."

"Well, I'm not happy." Chloe waved her hands. "We were supposed to help each other plan our weddings."

"I'll need your help with a reception." Piper stood and crossed to Chloe and grabbed her hands. "Plus, with you getting married soon, we'll have lots to do planning the wedding of your dreams."

"I've been thinking a remote wedding in the mountains would be nice." Chloe wrapped her arm around Piper's back and turned to Jake. "Maybe flying everyone into the cabin that brought us together?"

"Whatever makes you happy, makes me happy." Jake's lip twitched on one side as he stared up at Chloe.

Derrick glanced at Davis and rolled his eyes. Davis pretended to gag, making Derrick laugh. Maybe getting all lovey-dovey wasn't such a good idea. Besides, rescuing and rehabilitating abused horses and providing security for the rich kept him more than fulfilled. Having a relationship would just muck things up.

Don't miss the next adventure for the Stryker Security Force. Convincing Derrick will leave you on the edge of your seat! If you enjoyed Rafe and Chloe's story, please consider leaving a review.

ALSO BY SARA BLACKARD

Vestige in Time Series

Vestige of Power

Vestige of Hope

Vestige of Legacy

Vestige of Courage

Stryker Security Force Series

Mission Out of Control

Falling For Zeke

Capturing Sosimo

Celebrating Tina

Crashing Into Jake

Discovering Rafe

Convincing Derrick

Honoring Lena (coming July 2021)

SARA BLACKARD

MISSION
OUT OF
CONTROL

STRYKER SECURITY FORCE SERIES - PREQUEL

It was a mission like any other ... until it blew apart
around them.

When the Army's Special Ops team is tasked with
infiltrating the Columbian jungle and rescuing a
kidnapped State Department family, the mission seems
like every other one they've executed. But as the assignment unravels, not only is the mission's success at stake,
but all the brothers-in-arms leaving the jungle alive hangs
in the balance.

*Mission Out of Control is the prequel short story for
both Vestige in Hope and the Stryker Security Force
Series.*

ABOUT THE AUTHOR

Sara Blackard is a Christian romance novelist who writes stories that thrill the imagination and strum heartstrings. She's been a writer since she was able to hold a pencil. When she's not crafting wild adventures and sweet romances, she's homeschooling her five children, keeping their off-grid house running, or enjoying the Alaskan lifestyle she and her husband love.

Made in the USA
Monee, IL
15 February 2021

60547216R00125